Praise for *Hot Season*

"A beautiful book that asks the crucial question, is it worse to destroy a dam or to destroy a river? Which is to say, how do we live our conscience on a crowded, corrupted planet?."

—Monica Drake, author of *The Folly of Loving Life*

"*Hot Season,* Susan DeFreitas's finely wrought debut novel, explores the charged terrain where the youthful search for identity meets environmental activism and the romantic, illicit lure of direct action. A compelling book."

—Cari Luna, Oregon Book Award winner,
author of *The Revolution of Every Day*

"Susan DeFreitas's provocative novel asks big questions—not only about water rights and the importance of riparian corridors in the West, but about what it means to fight for the natural world. Young and idealistic, her characters are vulnerable, intricately rendered, and utterly engaging. *Hot Season* is a knockout."

—Michaela Carter, author of *Further Out Than You Thought*

"In Susan DeFreitas's riveting debut, the desert landscape looms large over the dreams and desires of three friends contending with big questions—such as who to love, who to trust, and what to sacrifice for the greater good. A tale of youth, lust, and activism, *Hot Season* is a beguiling college novel in the tradition of *The Secret History*."

—Mo Daviau, author of *Every Anxious Wave*

"The characters of Susan DeFreitas's exuberant new novel populate the American Southwest with wit and pathos. Half collegiate romp and half impassioned plea, *Hot Season* is a heartfelt debut that will grip readers with the fervor of first love."

—Jamie Duclos-Yourdon, author of *Froelich's Ladder*

Hot Season

A novel

By

Susan DeFreitas

Harvard Square Editions
New York
2016

Hot Season, by Susan DeFreitas

Cover image by Lucy Wu of Nine Gates Photography (www.ninegatesphotography.com), part of a series entitled "Forces of Nature."

Cover design by Gigi Little

Sections of this novel appeared as short stories in the following: "The Circus on Second Street"—*Weber: The Contemporary West* (Spring 2014); *Pyrophitic*—ELJ Publications (Afternoon Shorts, 2014); "Dead Man's Revival"—*Milkfist* (Fall 2015).

ISBN 978-1-941861-28-8
Printed in the United States of America

Published in the United States by
Harvard Square Editions
www.harvardsquareeditions.org

For the collective
2004–2006

"To live outside the law, you must be honest."

—Bob Dylan, "Absolutely Sweet Marie"

"...you must live a certain way, and do it swiftly, elegantly, because this is a desert, this water is only here, and then a hundred miles of nothing."

—Craig Childs, *The Secret Knowledge of Water*

Prologue

The Circus on Second Street

Katie

WHEN KATIE MET HUCKLEBERRY, he was juggling on the curb at the end of Second Street with a rose between his teeth. In that dented bowler hat, busted-out corduroy vest, and those dirty Carhartts—held together by nothing more, it seemed, than the patches attached to them—he looked like some handsome sideshow hobo, circa 1920. Which is to say, he looked like Katie's future bohemian lover.

She sidled up beside him, cast him what she hoped was a scandalous glance, and said, "Boy, did you run away with the circus?"

He smiled, revealing a slight gap between two front teeth.

Katie had always dreamed of having a bohemian lover. Not a boyfriend—she'd had a number of those—but a lover: the kind of person artists and revolutionaries casually introduced to friends at parties. And not the kind of wannabe frat parties that had characterized her high school years in the White Mountains, but rather, the kind where beautiful people wearing nothing but various shades of bright acrylic paint might discuss the failures of some noted political theorist while passing around a spliff, the way they did in Europe.

Katie had assumed that any institution of higher ed offering such courses as *Chomsky: Manufacturing Dissent* and *Ecological Issues in Site-Specific Dance* would pretty much guarantee her entrée into such a scene. But during her first month at Deep Canyon College in Crest Top, Arizona, she'd encountered nothing more than your run-of-the-mill college keggers and potlucks in crappy houses—such as this one here at the end of Second Street, where some unfortunate furniture had been hauled out into the front yard.

The boy launched two juggling pins up overhead, caught them behind his back with one hand, and then tossed the third and final pin high in the air. It flashed yellow-green through the cloudless blue and landed on his outstretched foot—stalled, miraculously, on his big toe.

His feet were filthy.

Somehow even that seemed charming.

"You know," she told her boho beau, "I've always wanted to learn how to juggle."

Juggling, until that very moment, had fallen somewhere between spelunking and chinchilla breeding in terms of Katie's general interests. But this boy was so intent on what he was doing, so deeply into it, that she wanted to be into it too.

He plucked the rose from between his teeth, holding it lightly between two fingers. "There's a show tonight," he told her. "A benefit for the Greene. You should come."

"Where at?"

He lifted his chin, as if this was a given. "The Black Cat."

What was the Greene, and why did it need benefitting? And where, exactly, was the Black Cat? Before Katie could embarrass herself by asking—or embarrass herself further, as she probably had bits of baba ghanoush from lunch gummed up between her teeth—she spied the sign beside them, half-hidden by the weedy trees. The Black Cat was this house, here at the end of Second Street, beside the entrance to the bike trail that ran along the creek.

"Cool," she said, in a manner intended to convey the same. "I'm Katie, by the way."

"Huckleberry."

Huckleberry held that long-stemmed red rose for a moment, his wrist turned elegantly out, and for a moment she thought he might present it to her—or at least extend his hand. Instead, he tucked the rose into his breast pocket and winked, or perhaps just blinked. Then he kicked the pin on his foot high overhead and started the same routine all over again.

* * *

Katie spent an hour or so that evening arranging and rearranging her hair, applying foundation and eyeliner and mascara and scrubbing it off again. She stood before herself now in the mirror, barefaced but for lip gloss, in the messy updo she'd settled on.

The tight V-neck was too low-cut—it made her look like she was trying too hard. She shrugged out of it and into a black turtleneck, which was more artsy, but too East Coast. Finally, she dug around in her dresser for that soft, familiar cotton T-shirt, a souvenir of the circus from the summer she was twelve, the summer her father had taken her to see Ringling Brothers and Barnum and Bailey in New York. On this shirt a silkscreened elephant teetered atop a tiny chair, juggling with a blond majorette who Katie had always thought looked like her but skinnier. The image seemed appropriate, considering, but who could say what was appropriate for an event such as this?

Or even what this event really was.

She could have asked her roommate Jenna for advice, but Jenna was beautiful—all she ever wore was jeans and flannels, and guys hit on her all the time. Jenna, the straight-A soil science major in her second semester, whom Katie's mom had loved. For her laugh, maybe, the way everyone did, but also for her secondhand knickknacks and potholders and slotted spoons and whatever else her mother had been terrified Katie would have to do without these three thousand miles from home.

The fact that Deep Canyon didn't have dorms had been a sticking point, as had the neighborhood, which was perhaps a bit seedy (Katie preferred to think of it as diverse). Her mom just couldn't seem to figure out why Katie hadn't applied to Columbia or Brown or even Barnard, like all her friends' kids back in Boston. Just like she couldn't seem to figure out how, after Mozart for Babies, Toddler Soccer, and a decade's worth of after-school programs, Katie had never managed to win an award of any type, never distinguished herself in any way except by acting in a few school plays and painting one fairly realistic portrait of Georgia O'Keeffe.

Her mom, who'd moved them all to New Hampshire so she could fulfill her life's dream of running for the Senate—to Whitefield, so Katie could attend the best school in what her parents clearly considered (though would never say) was a backwater state. Katie had taken to the mountains there and decided early on that her life's dream was simply to live among bigger ones, wilder ones, in the saturated colors of the Southwest that O'Keeffe had loved.

And now here she was, setting sail on her bike through the blue wash of twilight, with the flaming ruins of a sunset over that big butte to the west, through just the sort of colors she'd dreamed: indigo rose and magenta gold, cobalt and cadmium and even the hint of something green in between. With such colors stretched out overhead, everything back home seemed unreal—the little towns with their fussy flowers, the centennial farms with their brass plaques, the suburbs and cities ruled by cars, and above it all, the flat gray clouds pressing down.

Katie rolled past the little house bounded by leaning sunflowers, the string of Tibetan prayer flags lifting gently from its porch, past the Hispanic dudes barbecuing off the back of a pickup truck in the parking lot of their apartment building. The old guy who always sat out in front of his trailer smoking Old Golds lifted a hand to her as she passed, and she waved back, weaving her way through a tangle of kids on bikes; they called good-natured obscenities to one another, ignoring her. This was her neighborhood, her mountain town, her funky

Shangri-La. Barely two months had passed since she'd landed, but already it felt like home.

Autumn in the high desert didn't smell the way it did back home, but in the gathering dusk, something in it was the same: The wind in her face, increasingly crisp, the dry leaves crunching beneath her tires. Small shadows darting away at the periphery of vision, melding with the stuff of the mind. October now, coming on Halloween, and she could feel it—the sense that something new was possible.

Up ahead, round orange lanterns had been hung from the trees, a glowing constellation of moons. A crowd had gathered on the broken-down couches and easy chairs in front of the house at the end of the street; the sagging front porch was now a stage.

Katie pulled to a stop as quietly as she could and leaned her bike against a pileup of cruisers beside the fence. Moving gingerly through the crowd, she made her way to an open spot in the front yard and settled cross-legged in the dirt. A thin girl in an old-fashioned striped bathing suit and black skullcap stood at the head of the front-porch steps, cradling a ukulele.

This was the very tall, flat-chested girl with the Olive-Oyl hair Katie had seen somewhere on campus eating with chopsticks from a container of sprouts, looking lonely and awkward and odd. But then the girl struck a chord on the ukulele and started into singing, her voice high and tinny like a Smithsonian recording, and suddenly she was beautiful.

Katie recognized faces in the crowd, but no one she knew well enough to approach. She found herself scanning for Huckleberry—casually at first, but then in earnest. The only bowler in evidence belonged to a guy with a dark unibrow, taped-together glasses, and an anxious expression. Her eye kept snagging on him in the crowd, and she realized now he was watching her.

As quietly as possible, Katie extracted herself from the audience, stuffed a dollar in the jug marked *Save the Greene*

(Wondering, was that the campus commons, maybe? The little creek out back?) and made her way through the weedy trees, past the orange lanterns and the fairy lights, down a path composed of broken concrete and mosaics, into the still and the dark.

She thought maybe the lights were from a party next door, but then the grainy interplay of light and dark resolved itself into what appeared to be an old Super 8 movie playing in a shed behind the house.

The galvanized metal shed proved empty except for a series of grotesques: A big gray fish with whiskers of twisted wire lay across the concrete floor, its mouth open, dead black X's for eyes. A papier-mâché lizard with round toes—a salamander?—reared out of a backpack in a way that struck Katie as highly unnatural; it looked as if it was engaged in a tortured yoga pose. A flock of foam frogs with surprised eyes hovered on wires beside the door, holding little signs that said *Got Water?* A spectral projection played on a sheet rigged up on the far wall.

Katie leaned into the doorframe. The projector clicked beside her, running through footage from what seemed some sort of protest. A swarm of people chanted soundlessly, holding signs: *No Globalization Without Representation* and *No Farms No Food.* They surged forward, only to be thrown back by police in riot gear. The protesters retreated in a rush; one large, elderly woman who might have been Katie's kindergarten teacher fell and was lost in the crowd, and the whole thing started over again.

A branch snapped behind her. Katie turned to find a young man in a hoodie standing in the shadow of the tree beside the shed.

"Hey," she said, shivering. She still forgot sometimes how fast the temperature dropped after dark in Crest Top.

"I believe the footage is from Seattle."

It took her a moment to realize he was referring to the film playing inside the shed.

"Awesome," she said. Except, obviously, it wasn't; in this footage, people were getting blasted with tear gas. She tried again. "What's up with the puppets?"

The young man stepped into the light of the doorway, and now she could see that he wasn't a young man at all—he wore his hoodie oversized, like a student, but his hair had all gone gray. He was hardly taller than she was, slight of frame, with bright blue eyes. As he moved closer, she noticed that he was careful to maintain a respectful distance, mindful of her space. "The puppets are for the protest," he said.

"The protest?"

"To save the Greene."

Hadn't she seen something on a flyer in the mailroom about a protest on Monday? Something about a critically endangered catfish? "Is that," she said, "kind of a big deal around here?"

"It *is* kind of a big deal," he told her, as if this was some very intelligent question on her part. "Have you ever been to the headwaters of the Greene River?"

"No. I just got here, actually."

"To Crest Top? Or Arizona?"

"Both." The word came out almost breathlessly, a kind of confession.

"Well, then." He smiled. "Welcome."

Katie found herself unaccountably moved by this. It was the first time anyone besides her student orientation leader had welcomed her to Crest Top.

"To tell you the truth," he said, "I think the headwaters of the Greene River is one of the most beautiful places on earth."

"No shit."

This too was not the right thing to say. Katie knew it, but she didn't know why. Was it because she was already supposed to know all this? (But how could she, possibly? Wasn't there some point before everyone knew the things that made them cool, no matter how cool they were?)

The man's face had settled into softness. "Driving north toward Paulden, it's just this dry brown ranchland. Then you hang a right on Angus Road and turn down a little two track and all of it turns to green. Before long, you're surrounded by these giant cottonwood trees. Huge blue dragonflies cruise the corridor. Herons, kingfishers, golden eagles, swifts. All kinds of birds. All kinds of everything."

"That sounds amazing."

"It is amazing."

Katie looked off into the darkness. This odd little man had painted a picture in her mind that she loved, or wanted to love. She cleared her throat. "So, what's up with the river?"

"The city wants to drain it."

Her expression must have made it clear: she had no idea how such a thing was even possible.

"There are some people who've made a lot of money building houses in Crest Top," he explained. "They'd like to keep on building houses, but there's a law now that says they can't unless they find another hundred years' worth of water."

Katie nodded, nodded, nodded, as if enthusiasm and understanding were pretty much the same thing.

"Given the size of the aquifer that feeds the Greene, they could put in another hundred thousand homes if the Wind Valley Pipeline went through." The man was looking at her now like he expected a reply, but she just stood there stupidly, like the tree beside them. Finally, he said, "That would effectively double the size of the city."

Katie thought of her bike ride that evening—her little mountain town—and then flashed on the sprawling developments north of Phoenix she'd glimpsed on the ride up from the airport with her mom. "It seems like that would sort of suck."

He chuckled. "You know what? There are a lot of us who agree with you. That's why we started this place." He lifted a hand toward the house behind them—the house that was not a house, where the street ended and the creek began. "So people could come together to oppose the pipeline, to raise funds and organize, the way we are tonight."

A fleet of moths had gathered in the beam of the projector, obscuring the footage in the course of its latest loop. For a few seconds, Katie and this little man, whose name she did not know, stood together in the fluttering half light, which seemed to have softened the expressions of the puppets. That critically endangered catfish looked as if it could have been sleeping; the salamander might simply have been caught in the process of standing up; the round white eyes of the frogs looked off into the darkness beyond the shed, as if they could see something that Katie and the man beside her could not.

He blinked as a moth landed on his cheek. "I'm sorry," he said. "My name is Dyson."

"Katie."

He smiled. Dyson had kind eyes that drooped at the edges, like her father's. "It's good to know you, Katie."

The way Dyson said it, she felt like he really meant it—that she, in particular, was a good person to know. The white moth that had landed on his cheek sat still, unmoving, and it gave him an air of strangeness, of wisdom. He seemed about to tell her something, something important, standing there in the doorway, when the roof compressed and decompressed in sharp little pops and cracks above them. Something heavy was walking along the spine of the shed.

Huckleberry, bowler in hand, dropped to the earth beside them. Then he rose to his feet and flicked the brim of his hat up along the inside of one arm, into the crook of an elbow, and—in one fluid motion—up and onto his head.

"Huck," said Dyson. "Nice of you to drop in."

Huck acknowledged this poor pun with a dubious look. He turned to Katie and touched the brim of his bowler.

"I take it you're acquainted," Dyson said.

"Mildly." Huck smiled. "Very mildly."

Katie had the feeling Huckleberry could tell her updo, casually mussed, had in fact been the end product of various failed attempts in front of the mirror that evening. Her Levis seemed suddenly too tight, her child-sized T-shirt seasonally inappropriate.

"Are you coming with us to the protest?" Huckleberry asked.

"Maybe." She hesitated. "I have class."

Huckleberry glanced at Dyson and grinned that gap-toothed grin, and the whiff of condescension was as palpable as a sudden pocket of humidity. Katie wondered, how old was Huck? Twenty-two? Twenty-four? Not so much older than she was, really, and yet it was clear here he considered her some kind of kid.

"Maybe I could still help. If you need, like, volunteers."

It was as if she had not spoken. Dyson had fixed those piercing blue eyes on Huck, even as that white moth still clung to his cheek, its tiny black eyespots unmoving. Did he know it was there? Did he not? One way or the other, he'd made no move to remove it, and it was starting to make her feel uncomfortable, that moth. Katie had the inexplicable urge to step closer to Dyson, to brush it away.

"I left you a little something," he told Huck.

"What's the occasion?" Huck asked.

"No occasion."

Huckleberry held Dyson's gaze, and for a long moment it felt like the part in a Western movie where the hero and his sidekick give each other one last look—communicating, wordlessly, something deep in the cowboy code—before turning to face off against the bad guys.

But something in the way Huck looked at Dyson made her wonder: Who was the hero here, and who was the sidekick?

And who, exactly, were the bad guys?

The projector click, click, clicked through its footage, and the protesters advanced then retreated, advanced then retreated. The little man with her father's eyes made a gentle motion, as if wiping away a tear, and the white moth flew off into the night.

Whatever was going on here had nothing to do with her. But Katie wasn't willing to leave these guys alone to talk about whatever it was they weren't talking about because she was there. Through the branches of the tree beside them, the harvest moon hung swollen and golden, like a moon in a movie. On the front-porch stage, someone spoke, and the audience erupted into laughter.

Katie thought of her friends back home. They were probably in their dorm rooms right now, blowing dirtweed into a Pringles can stuffed with dryer sheets, the way they had in high school. Or hanging out at those loud house parties they used to crash at UNH, doing their best to look sexy. Whereas she, Katie, was here at this bohemian benefit thing full of beautiful people—people who were beautiful not because they were trying to be beautiful but because they believed in something.

She wanted to tell Huck and Dyson how cool it was that they were using puppets at a protest—about how she'd once acted in a stage production of *Silent Spring*—about how her whole family was hardcore into saving the earth. The night, the sky, that big ol' moon, whatever; if she didn't say something soon, she'd disappear. Finally, she turned to Huckleberry and said, "Where'd you come from?"

"Me?" He fingered the back of an earlobe. "Ma'am, I come from Kentucky."

Dyson chuckled.

"No, I mean just now. How'd you get on top of the shed?"

Huckleberry simply opened his hand, as if releasing a dove, and looked up. In the branches of the tree above them was a tree house. It hung above the spot where they stood, just south of the golden moon.

"Are you fucking serious?"

Was there really even a little window up there—and a little potted plant on a windowsill? The image of it washed over her in some woozy déjà vu.

Huck cast a glance at Dyson. This time it seemed a kind of question, but Katie didn't care what the question was.

* * *

In volunteering to help Dyson at the Black Cat, Katie had assumed that Huckleberry would be there. But when she arrived on Thursday after class, the only people making puppets for the protest were Dyson himself, Olive Oyl (the girl she'd seen on the front-porch stage, whose name was Trinity), Unibrow (the other boy who'd been wearing a bowler that night, whose name was Jonas), and a standoffish girl with bleach-blond, punked-out hair named Michelle. They were set up in the front yard, dipping strips of newspaper into buckets of papier-mâché and pasting them onto the chicken-wire frame of a giant backpack puppet. The mâché was only flour and water, but it was cold and slimy and looked like someone had puked up oatmeal. After half an hour or so, Katie half decided to bail.

Instead, she wandered the Black Cat, which looked like an anarchist lending library set up in someone's living room. Handmade zines were filed alongside paperbacks and hardcovers on shabby bookshelves that presided over various pouchy couches and easy chairs. Katie selected a book entitled *Art and Revolution* on a shelf between *Food Preservation for Everyone* and *Our Bodies, Ourselves*. She was signing her name and phone number on the clipboard at the self-service station when she glimpsed Dyson in the kitchen with Michelle.

Michelle was a figure drawn tight, folded into herself, elbows and cheekbones all set at sharp angles; the ring through her septum gave her child's face, oddly, the severity of late middle age. Dyson spoke to her in low, soothing tones. Something about the way the two of them stood, leaning against the counters, their proximity—were they a couple? Dyson must have been pushing fifty, and Michelle—how old was Michelle? Not much older than Katie. And yet, Katie understood, they lived here. The Black Cat was their place.

Back out front, Trinity and Jonas were working on a ragged raccoon composed of recycled produce boxes. They sat quietly beside their misshapen creature, their slender hands occasionally intersecting as they reached for a paintbrush. When Katie returned to her spot beside them, they looked up, thin-faced and startled, like deer.

Bike brakes squealed to a halt in the driveway, and there was Huck, towing a box labeled *Food Not Bombs*. Huck, in those same stained Carhartts, the same corduroy vest. He loosened the bungees from the bike trailer, hoisted the box aloft, and dazzled Katie with a smile before disappearing into the house.

"That boy ain't nothing but trouble."

This was from a girl with tanned, freckled skin stationed on the old sofa beside the porch. She and her friend were stuffing nylon pantyhose with soft foam. They wore their dreadlocks tied up in bright scarves like African queens.

"Why's that?" Katie asked her.

The girl with the freckles drew the pantyhose tight around the foam, twisting it shut like a garbage bag. "Because he's a boy."

"Duh." Her girlfriend grinned.

"You could save yourself some heartache, you know. Play for the home team." The girl with the freckles pulled a threaded needle through the pantyhose as she spoke, creating an indentation in the stuffed form. Personally, Katie didn't know if she had what it took to play for the home team, but she watched, transfixed, as the girl repeated the maneuver and two eye-sockets magically appeared in the flesh-colored nylon. She asked Katie if she wanted to help them, and Katie realized that she did.

Digging a set of paints out of the box of art supplies, she felt a kind of hum in her chest. Remembering the way she'd felt that day in the library when she'd discovered Georgia O'Keeffe's *One Hundred Flowers*. Remembering the way she'd felt as a kid, smearing slick globs of green and blue over a sheet of butcher paper. Katie had never won an art competition, not even in elementary school—had never even placed. So why did it feel like this was what she was supposed to do?

Her mother didn't understand that feeling. Her dad did, maybe, but he didn't want to see her struggle. What about when you were in college? she'd asked him. What about the civil rights marches? What about the war protests? What about the fight to save the Arctic, the monarch, the humpback whale? Wasn't anything really worthwhile a struggle?

It was true what she'd wanted to say that night, that her parents were hardcore into saving the earth. But saving the earth, for Katie's parents, was all about money—where they spent it and who they gave it to. They considered themselves liberals, but where the rubber met the road, her parents weren't so different from their conservative small-town neighbors, which was something Katie had come to understand when she'd been suspended for protesting her high school's dress code. Of course the dress code was sexist, but Katie didn't want that suspension on her permanent record, did she? Her mother had been on the school board at the time; she'd spent an hour in the principal's office, and that suspension had magically disappeared.

For as long as Katie could remember, her folks had talked about finding your calling, about your gifts and the needs of the world, etcetera and so forth. But as soon as Katie had brought up a major in fine art, it was all about job security and health insurance. All of it so canned it might as well have been recorded. Her father might have been different once, but that glimpse of the circus they'd had that summer, when he'd told her she could do anything, be anyone, was a distant memory.

Hence, Katie's major in environmental science, which her folks considered a safer bet. Like parenthood had been a pretty serious gamble for them and they'd already lost more than they'd planned to spend.

Katie had always thought things would have been different if her parents really believed in her. But it occurred to her as she worked—as she began to shape her own soft form—maybe that wasn't even the problem. Maybe the problem, when it came right down to it, was that her parents didn't really believe in their own beliefs.

* * *

She caught a glimpse of Huck a few times after that, once in the kitchen of the Cat, cooking dinner with Michelle, and once out by the creek, smoking a joint with the old hippie guy who was carving a stump back there. Both times, Katie waited around to talk to Huck, but the moment never seemed right. And what was she going to say, anyway?

Still, if Katie didn't make a move soon, Huck would forget all about the day they'd met, when she'd asked him if he'd run away with the circus—if he hadn't forgotten already. But what about that smile, the day he'd arrived at the Cat on his bike? And what was going on with him and Dyson? She lay awake thinking about it, twisting the blankets around her into a kind of cocoon.

The next morning she bummed a joint off her roommate, walked down to the Cat, and waited around all day for Huck to show up. Toward sunset, when she was just about to give up, she spotted him on the front porch talking to a girl with green hair. This girl wasn't beautiful, necessarily, but Katie felt a needle of jealousy. Huck lifted a hand in Katie's direction through the doorway, and she waved back. But there was no way to approach him while he was talking to this person.

Katie stood to reshelf the book she'd been reading, and when she turned back, both Huck and the girl were gone.

She caught up with him as he was dumping leftover papier-mâché in the compost bin out back. "Psst, Huck," she said. "I've got a proposition for you."

He cast her a sidelong glance.

"I've got some seedless Humboldt rolled up in my pocket." Katie leaned in closer. "I'll smoke you out if you show me your tree house."

They stood for a moment beside the stinking compost pile in the descending dusk, the slick mass of papier-mâché between them. Whether Huck was considering her offer or her personally, Katie couldn't tell.

"All right," he said. "It's a deal." It took her a second to realize he was offering her his hand. She reached out and shook it, and there they were, shaking, like Bugs and Daffy in the dark.

* * *

Katie stood in the backyard of the Cat that night watching Huckleberry ascend the tree. He grabbed hold of the lowest branch and then swung up and caught the next behind his knees like a trapeze artist. From there he sat up, grasped a higher branch, and swung out onto the platform of the tree house. A moment later he let down a rope ladder, and a little thrill passed through her, like a bass beat.

The tree house was smaller inside than she'd imagined. By the light of a Coleman lantern hung from a nail she could see a little shelf with a couple of books on it: *Jonathan Livingston Seagull* and *A Natural History of the Intermountain West.* An internal-frame backpack lay propped against a wall, and next to it, a guitar case. All Huckleberry seemed to possess by way of furniture was a futon mattress covered by a well-worn quilt, and an old steamer trunk.

What did you expect? Katie asked herself. *A kitchen table?*

He was watching her, she realized. Not in a you're-so-pretty way, but not in a bad way either.

"This is awesome," she said, plopping down on the mattress. "Did you build this place?"

"Me and Dyson."

Katie leaned back and rummaged in her jeans pocket. "You don't have a lighter, do you?"

"Maybe." He popped the latch on the steamer trunk and felt along its lining. "No worries." And quicker than thought he was out the door, dropping onto the roof of the shed. From the tree-house window, Katie watched him disappear into the Black Cat.

Huck's quilt was composed of fraying denim panels covered in an intricate tree that must have taken someone hours to embroider. The denim was marked up in Sharpie with what appeared to be peoples' names: *Nolie, Scatch, Erik the Redd, Lillith, Foghorn, Unis*. His crew from who knows where.

Moths flittered helplessly around the lantern, and Katie realized the steamer trunk was still propped open.

She found a few old notebooks inside, some yellowed love letters in looping cursive, and some photographs of a younger Huck with a lady who must have been his mom. There were letters in Spanish too, a paper from some long-ago class at the University of Oregon, and a handful of newspaper clippings about a dam in southern Washington that had been decommissioned following "catastrophic damage." All this had been shoved to one side of two cardboard boxes, which were full of old zines. Though their edges were dog-eared, their Xeroxed print was still bold and clear.

All the zines were consecutive issues of a single title, *Caterwaul*—page after page, all in the same all-caps handwriting, typewriter type, and photocopied illustrations. *Caterwaul* contained a guide to eating free in most major U.S. cities, legal information for avoiding arrest, and a basic bike repair primer, along with what appeared to be internal memos from various oil and timber companies. Katie glanced around—Huck still seemed occupied down below—before digging deeper into the stacks. There she found issue number fifty-four, a special edition with a special heading: *How to Set Fires Using Electrical Timers.*

In the light of the lantern, Katie scanned the pages. Those directions looked so innocuous, like the steps of a science experiment. But this sort of science was not at all safe.

No, she decided, her parents wouldn't have liked it at all.

Katie flipped through the pages of illustrations, remembering high school chemistry, the colors of the flames on the Bunsen burner, blue and yellow and pale lemon-green. The sense that certain basic elements in fact wanted to explode. This recipe wanted to explode, over and over again, in different places and at different times, and maybe it already had.

She placed the special edition of *Caterwaul* carefully back in order with the others, shut the trunk, and settled on the bed. A moment later Huckleberry swung soundlessly back in through the door.

"Come on," he said. "I'll take you up top."

* * *

Smoking a joint in Huck's tree house was one thing—it wasn't actually that far off the ground, and there was that rope ladder. But getting high on a platform at the top of the tree? Just the thought of it made her queasy. There was something amazing up there Huck just had to show her, so she didn't feel like she could refuse, but even if she managed to get up there, how on earth was she going to get down?

For a moment, clinging to a limb, Katie thought she might faint. But Huckleberry was patient, offering his hand or even sometimes his knee as a step when she couldn't reach the next branch. Eventually they arrived at a packing pallet tied to the tree with a thick length of red climbing rope. A North Face bag lay spread out on top, and Katie settled on it with relief.

"Is this where you sleep at night?"

"Unless it's raining."

She decided to take that as a yes, as it had yet to rain since she'd arrived in Crest Top at the start of the semester. Venturing a look back down at the way they'd come, she was amazed to discover how simple it was—just two steps, really, and the light through the back window of the Cat clearly illuminated the way, once she let her eyes adjust. What had she been so afraid of?

Huckleberry handed her the lighter; she sparked off the joint and took a long drag before handing it to him. She grinned. "You're pretty good at climbing trees."

He licked a finger and moistened a spot where the bright red cherry was running. "I used to live in a tree."

"A different tree?"

"A bigger tree."

"Where?"

He exhaled the word: "Headwaters."

It came back to her, from her Environmental Justice seminar that semester—Julia Butterfly Hill, the activist who'd protested the clear-cutting of Headwaters National Forest. Julia Butterfly Hill, who'd used climbing equipment to make her home high in the branches of a redwood tree, supported by other activists, for 208 days straight.

Julia Butterfly Hill—even her name—had always seemed, to Katie, impossibly brave and beautiful. Like Dian Fossey, or Gandhi, even. But sitting there with Huckleberry, Katie could see how simple it must have been, how peaceful. To just decide what you stand for and refuse to come down.

"Was it quiet up there?"

"Aside from the chainsaws."

Katie blinked, her contacts fogging. "I'd love to live in a tree."

Huckleberry was staring off into the darkness now.

"When I was a kid, I used to climb this one tree," Katie told him. "Just in my folks' backyard, but sometimes I used to sit up there and pretend I was an owl and that the day was really night, but I could see because I had super-owl night vision."

Huckleberry nodded, but it didn't seem like he was really listening. It seemed like he was scanning the perimeter, far off, for the approach of some enemy unknown.

"Did you climb trees in Kentucky?" she asked him.

"My mom tells me I climbed most anything around."

She thought maybe he'd go on then, but he didn't. So she just sat beside him in the dark, on a packing pallet strapped to a tree, high on Humboldt greenbud, thinking of Huckleberry, high in his redwood tree. Unencumbered by parental expectations. His folks probably thought he was doing great. They were probably behind him all the way.

"So what do you do for…" She couldn't think of a good way to ask what he did for money.

"Street performing, mostly."

"Did you always know you wanted to do that? Like, deep down?"

He kept quiet a moment. "Not exactly."

"But it's cool, right?"

"Cool enough."

"Have you and Dyson been friends a long time?"

"Katie."

"Yeah?"

"Check it out."

Huckleberry lay back on the sleeping bag. She lay down beside him, careful to touch him only a little, and only in a way that was clearly accidental. She blinked.

The Milky Way was so distinct through the branches above them that Katie thought at first it was a cloud, hazy and drifting through the night. But there were no clouds and there was no humidity—nothing in between them and the vast vault of the heavens but miles of empty air.

"That's…" She reached for a word.

"Rent's not bad either."

She laughed at this, feeling comfortable, just lying there beside him in the dark, not touching. But then another moment passed and it made her want to scream.

For all her bohemian fantasies, for all her bold moves, Katie wanted more than a lover—Katie wanted love. And yet, she realized, there were limits to what she would do for it. She might flirt with a boy she had only just met; she might lie, just a little, to get his attention. She might insinuate herself into his world by pretending to care about the things he cared about, although she didn't know enough yet about those things to actually care about them. She might even bum a joint off her roommate, wait around all day for him to show up, and invite herself up to his place to smoke it. But she would not take his hand, lying next to him in the dark. She would not kiss him first. Somehow, just knowing this about herself made her feel better.

"I saw a guitar down there," she said.

"Yes, ma'am."

"Do you sing?"

In the dark, she could feel him smile.

"Well, then, why don't you?"

Huckleberry cleared his throat, and for a moment she thought he'd produce some excuse. But then he pulled in a breath, like a breeze through the branches, and her heart lifted. He began to sing.

The song was one she knew, by Gillian Welch. A song that, for Katie, had always been like a letter from home—not the home where she'd grown up but the home to which she was headed. It was a long song, and in the way Huckleberry returned, time and again, to the chorus, she could hear in it the circular rhythms of traveling and hiking and sitting in the woods by yourself for days and months on end. *I dream a highway back to you, love...*

If this song were a color, it would have been the blue wash of twilight tinged with red. If this song were a shape, it would have been a spiral, returning to itself in different ways, over and over again.

Gillian Welch's husky whiskey voice and raw clawhammer banjo had sustained Katie through bouts of heartache and homesickness and crushing self-doubt that semester. She'd put on *Revelator* sometimes late at night and smear the canvas with the ugliest colors she could find—dark browns and yellows and pinks—until she didn't feel scared anymore. Until she could feel her parents' fear of their childhood poverty, her own fear of her own mediocrity, break apart inside her and dissolve.

Katie knew it was not really her that Huckleberry was singing to, but it didn't matter. For the time it took him to sing this song, she was the girl he loved, the girl with the cursive handwriting who'd written the letters in the old trunk in his tree house.

When the song ended, its blues and reds bled back into the darkness.

Katie thought he might kiss her then. Or take her hand. But he didn't. So she lay there beside him in the dark that was coming on cold, and would soon be freezing, under the stars, which seemed suddenly cliché, with her hands shoved deep in her pockets and her toes going numb.

A part of her thought, *It's okay. We're just getting to know each other.* But another part of her understood, intuitively, this was as close as they would ever come.

* * *

The pipeline protest came and went. Trinity and Jonas officially became an item, and Katie hooked up with a boy from her Environmental Justice seminar. Over Thanksgiving break, she had a fight with her mom about the war, of all things, and then, to make matters worse, the networks called Ohio for Bush.

Katie returned to Crest Top early on a Saturday morning laced with frost. She let herself in with her key and made her way upstairs to her room, only to find those two cardboard boxes from Huckleberry's trunk sitting on her bed. Beside it lay a single, wilted rose.

Katie lived on the second floor of the house she shared with Jenna. Jenna, as far as she knew, was still asleep. The house had been locked when she'd arrived, and she did not recall having left her window open.

Katie stepped into the cold air pouring in through that window and studied the tangle of branches outside. Those branches, she could see, hung over a long drainpipe, which might be accessible, for the right person, from the ground.

Then Jenna was clomping up the stairs behind her. "Hey," Katie said.

"Katie, did you hear?" Forget the hugs, the hi, the big welcome home—Katie's roommate stood there in her boyfriend's T-shirt and boxers in the doorway, gnawing a fingernail.

"Hear what?" The rest of Jenna's nails, Katie could see, had already been whittled to the nub.

"The FBI raided the Black Cat last night."

Katie turned back to the boxes on her bed. Remembering those timber-company memos, that special issue number fifty-four.

"They say that guy Dyson blew up a dam."

"What?"

"He's on the run. They're calling everyone on the Cat's mailing list." Jenna lowered her voice. "Are you—I mean, are we on their mailing list?"

Katie nodded slowly, feeling the pieces of everything in motion falling down around her. That look Huck and Dyson had exchanged, like cowboys—like the good guys headed into a showdown. They'd known.

"Katie?"

Katie shut her eyes. Remembering Huck, that day they'd met, on the curb in front of the Cat. The way he'd smiled at her. Out of everyone in this town, she was the one he had trusted with those zines. He'd known she'd know what to do with them. And she did.

She could see it all in her mind's eye, unfolding: She would load up those boxes in the milkcrate on the back of her bike. She'd roll over the cracked concrete of her neighborhood, past Second Street and up the hill to school. She'd climb the stairs to the obscure third floor of the Deep Canyon College library, balancing one box of *Caterwaul* on each hand, with that wilted rose between her teeth.

She would take those dog-eared zines and place them gently on a shelf between back issues of the old *Earth Uprising Journal* and the *Early American Train Circus*, or whatever was filed beside it. There she would pause and take Huckleberry's rose from between her teeth. She would place it delicately behind her ear.

No one would be there to observe this, but in that moment, she would be beautiful.

And when they called her, if they called her—this ominous *they*, with their tired routine—Katie would tell them she'd met Dyson Lathe, or whatever his name was, at a party once like everyone else. If they inquired about Huck, she would tell them she'd never known anyone by that name. And she would look these people in the eye as she said it. She would say the words with such conviction that even she would believe it.

One

Pyrophitic

Rell

WINTERS IN CREST TOP were generally mild, despite the altitude. That was one of the things Rell liked about her college town, the way snow was no more than a novelty, a snow-globe fantasy of soft, swirling flakes that melted away the next day like a dream. But the winter of her senior year snapped hard and cold, with temps in the teens, and brought so much snow that it shut the town down. She was almost happy to go home to Pittsburgh for the holidays, where at least the roads were plowed. But her boyfriend, Trevor, was increasingly vague on the phone, and by the time New Year's rolled around, Rell had begun to suspect that he hadn't driven to Mendocino to see his sister, the way he'd claimed—that he'd stayed in Crest Top instead.

Why? And why had he lied?

It was clear from the moment she walked in the door: Someone had left a peachy-pink windbreaker on the coatrack by the woodstove. Someone had left a bar of honeysuckle soap on the ceramic dish by the sink. Someone had been sleeping in *her* bed and cuddling with *her* cat and using *her* loofah to buff her butt, for all she knew.

That someone was Trina, a perky adventure education major with chiseled biceps. Trevor had been meaning to tell Rell about her, but he'd felt like Rell would be mad. Well, no shit, she wanted to say, and a few choice things as well, but it was all so immature and awkward and awful that her voice never made it past the hard lump that had formed in her throat. At that point, nothing she could have said would have made a difference anyway; the happy couple was long past the love-goggles stage and on to the type of passive-aggressive bickering that had taken Rell and Trevor years to achieve.

What she wanted more than anything then was her own space—a clear, sunny space with sweeping views where she could sit and sip her tea in the mornings. Counter space and sink space, free of Trevor's dishes; wall space and head space, free of his reggae posters and glassware, the sweet reek of his pot. A quiet space of her own where she could lay out the maps and cuttings associated with her senior thesis, which centered on those perverse plants of the Southwest that require fire to germinate.

But the breakup arrived at the beginning of January, which was the wrong time of year for space in Crest Top. Moreover, space cost the kind of money Trevor had but she did not. So Rell was forced to take up residence, in her final semester, in a room the size of a shoebox in a janky old rattrap in the barrio.

Which, for the record, was surrounded by all manner of noise—domestic altercations, house parties, shit-talking little eight-year-old hoods—and wholly lacking in views, unless you counted the two built-down mobile homes across the alley out back. There was a yard, at least, with space for a garden, which was something she'd wanted that Trevor had not, but the house itself was full of tacky linoleum and questionable carpet and had been rented by students so long no one had any idea who half the furniture in it belonged to. Fortunately for Rell, it was also so drafty that the two freshmen who'd signed the lease on the place were looking for a roommate in the off-season just to help them cover the heat.

Seven-thirty-seven Sycamore Street was a world away from the pimped-out cabins in the foothills of the Bradshaws favored by trust-fund babies and rock-jocks like Rell's ex. But Trevor and Trina were like smoke that spring: no matter where Rell went or what she did, she could not seem to avoid them.

Spring being the season when the Forest Service set the woods on fire. A control burn, they called it—a minor disaster now, while there was still snowmelt in the mountains, meant to stave off a major disaster later.

Trevor and Trina at the coffee shop, Trevor and Trina at the bar. Trevor and Trina on the campus commons, cinched in a skeezy liplock, flexing their firmly muscled forearms in an effort to bring themselves, impossibly, closer. Whenever Rell least expected it, the smell of smoke would find her, and she'd find herself blinking back tears.

She had studied the lifecycles of pyrophitic plants, even transected a quarter-mile section of the Bridal Creek Fire, which had nearly burned to the Crest Top city limits; she understood that what was happening out there was normal, necessary, even. And yet it pained her that spring, the way so many things that had taken so long to grow were dying.

Now here she sat on the back porch with her roommate Katie, who was all of eighteen, inhaling what was possibly the strongest rolling tobacco on the face of the earth. The organic American Spirit was even worse than the regular, and smoking it felt like being kicked by a horse. But this, they reasoned, was what kept them from smoking more than they did, so they kept on buying it.

"Apparently," Katie was confiding, "dude is a bit of a skank."

"Super skank, or just your average?"

"Probably just your average, but Jenna thinks he's, like, Mr. Romance."

It was the first real warm day of the year, and the old apple tree in the backyard was sizzling with drunken honeybees. It was too nice out to get any work done. Too nice out to do anything, it seemed, except lie around in the sun gossiping about their roommate's love life.

"It's a shame," Katie said. "Scott's such a nice guy."

Scott really was a nice guy. So nice he'd followed Jenna all the way across the country when she left for college. So nice he was training to be an emergency medical technician so he could help people professionally, he said—as in, for a living. When it came down to it, Scott wasn't even bad looking. It was just that he didn't drink or smoke or even swear, and he didn't really seem to get into much of anything besides running. Which he did, religiously, at six in the morning. So now Jenna and this new guy, whom she'd been spending a lot of time with at the bike shop at school, had started going out to the bars together too.

Rell took a drag off their cigarette, her eyes watering. "They say sometimes it's like a sneeze, right? If you hold out long enough, it goes away."

"Aren't you supposed to pinch your nose to stop a sneeze?" Katie asked. "Or push your tongue against the roof of your mouth?"

Rell passed the cigarette from the couch, loosening a chunk of stuffing from a hole in the upholstery. Katie took it and pulled a drag. "What if Scott's really, like, Jenna's soul mate?" she wondered. "What if she winds up blowing the love of her life for this Crockett dude, who winds up being a total skankfest?"

"Then she should take up running."

"But what if *Crockett* is really her soul mate? What if Jenna denies her connection with him and then spends the rest of her life wondering what they might have had?"

Rell found herself amazed sometimes by Katie's sheer credulity. The girl fell for someone new every day of the week, and she acted as if every crush was her last. To her, this wasn't a matter of doing your longtime boyfriend the simple courtesy of breaking up with him before screwing someone else. (Or hey, even *not* screwing someone else.) It was an infinitely tangled conundrum with no real solution.

Maybe this was why Rell had spent more time with Katie than any of her actual friends that spring—those ladies who, like Rell, had loved and lost and accrued an air of world-weary sophistication on the subject. Katie was a freshman, a romantic, a true believer in the sweet notion that any little spark of attraction could keep you warm for the rest of your life.

"Shh," Katie whispered. "He's right there."

"Who?"

"Dude."

A skinny, shirtless fellow in a floppy hat was making his way through their backyard, past the coils of chicken wire and their new garden beds. He had long brown hair and a goatee and was trailing what appeared to be an Alsatian. It followed along behind him on a length of rope as he made his way to their back-porch steps.

"Ladies," he said. "Beautiful day."

Rell shot Katie a look. "Is that—a goat?"

They were now eye level with the thing, and it was indeed a goat. With its cloven hooves, bulging belly, and slanted pupils, there was nothing else for it to be.

"This is Molly," he said. "Molly, meet—"

"Katie," said Katie.

"And Rell."

Molly, unimpressed, chewed her cud.

"And who might you be?" Rell knew very well who he was, but neither she nor Katie had been officially introduced.

"Crockett. At your service." Crockett removed his floppy hat and held it to his chest, like an old-time country suitor—an effect made ironic by his tattoo, which depicted a lion wearing a crown. It stared fiercely at them over the brim of his hat, waving its tricolor flag. "Molly and I were actually wondering if Jenna was around."

Again, Rell cast a glance at Katie. "Jenna's over at Scott's, isn't she?"

"Oh yeah." Katie twirled a strand of her highlights, its various shades of blond, in a supremely casual manner. "Haven't seen her around. We can tell her you stopped by, though."

"Cool."

Crockett fit his hat back on his head as if to leave, but then he just stood there at the foot of their steps grinning, like some kind of neighborhood stray—hoping for a warm bed, maybe, or a dish with his name on it. "If you don't mind me saying," he said, "I had no idea Jenna lived with such attractive women."

Out of the corner of her eye, Rell caught Katie smirking down at a couple of elm beetles making their way across the porch, their hind ends stuck together. In just the past few days, the entire town had become infested with these little black-and-red bugs, all doing their best to get laid.

"If you don't mind me saying," Rell said, "it looks like your goat is taking a crap." There was, in fact, no denying it: even as Rell spoke, little brown pellets were dropping to the ground to the aft of the goat.

Crockett shook his head. "Molly." His grin had turned sheepish, but he seemed less embarrassed than amused.

He walked over to the side of the shed, returned with their shovel, and then scooped that pile of pellets aloft and carried it over to the garden beds they'd prepared. He proceeded to work the manure in systematically, thoroughly, breaking up the hard clods of dirt they'd missed. Probably with more effort than strictly necessary.

The boy was so skinny that his belt barely held his pants up, and the tops of his boxers showed below his slim hips. But he was lithe and brown, and his muscles rippled as he worked, and there was no denying that he looked good—or that it felt good, sitting outside on a warm day in the spring, to watch a man break a sweat in the sun.

"Ladies," he said, "anything else I can do for you?"

"No," Katie said, "I think that'll do it."

Crockett smiled and tipped his hat. Then he turned, took the goat's lead, and made his way back down the alley.

Rell turned to Katie. She'd been about to make fun of the boy's hairless chest, the Lion of Judah tattooed there.

Instead, she let loose with a sneeze.

* * *

There was a funk DJ that night at Billy Jack's Bar and Grill, an event of some significance in Crest Top. Of perhaps equal significance, as far as Rell and Katie were concerned, was the prize for the Best Funk Freak.

Rell owned a pair of gold-lamé super bells, the genuine article, which had belonged to her mother. This was her first real night out since Trevor had left her for Trina, and clearly the prize was hers. Especially considering this cheap gold hairspray she'd snagged at the dollar store, which was no doubt toxic as hell but made her long brown hair, which she'd curled for the occasion, look as shiny and metallic as Barbarella's boobs. She emerged from a stinking cloud of the stuff to find Katie standing in the doorway in three-inch platforms, a white tube top, a purple wig, and long purple eyelashes.

"What do you think?" Katie asked, tugging up the top. "Too white trash?"

"Are you kidding?"

Rell could not help but laugh. Katie looked amazing.

Despite that little fimo-bead necklace she wore—signifying, ostensibly, her allegiance to the jam-band culture of the greater Northeast—Katie came across as super conventional, almost square, at a place like Deep Canyon College. Maybe it was those fussy salon highlights, her plaid button downs; maybe it was those boat shoes she favored, which could not help but look a bit lost in a town so high and dry. And yet, Rell could see, Katie had another side, which must have been in keeping with all those paintings in her room she would never let anyone in to see.

"Oh my goodness, y'all look *incredible*!"

That was Jenna, standing on the landing, wearing the same thing she always wore: pigtails, a flannel shirt, and her old Chuck Taylors. Jenna, with her adorable dimples—people always took her for a lightweight, but Rell had it on good authority she'd turned down an offer that fall at Duke.

"Is Scott coming?" Rell asked. Though of course she already knew.

"Not tonight," Jenna said. As if there was any night that Scott would be joining them. "But Crockett's going to be there!"

Rell and Katie shared a glance; inevitably, they agreed, the only one of them who currently had a boyfriend would be the first to get hit on.

They all climbed aboard Rell's old blue Volvo—a.k.a., the Vulva—and set off downtown. On the way, they tried to find some funk to play, but Elliott Smith was stuck in the Vulva's CD player, so Rell turned it off and they sang *she's a brick, hou-ouse*, raising the roof and clapping in time.

Billy Jack's was bumping with sweaty bodies in pleather trench coats, white-boy afros, and fake gold chains. The place was probably 50 percent over capacity and hot-boxed all to hell. Scanning the crowd, Rell was struck by a moment of irrational panic. But of course Trevor wasn't there. Trevor hated funk—and jazz and rap—and no one could talk him into any kind of anything he wasn't into.

Katie and Jenna flashed their smiles and their fake IDs at the door while Rell rummaged in her purse. The bouncer glanced up at her, his bald head reflecting the Fat Tire sign, and waved her through.

How many nights had she spent at Billy Jack's with Trevor? And how many mornings had she dragged herself out of bed to write papers on plant propagation and the ethnobotanical traditions of the Hopi? All the time Rell had spent in Crest Top seemed to have passed in a kind of dream.

Soon she'd be graduating, heading off to who knows where, starting her career—even now, it didn't quite feel real, but somehow she could see herself, years on down the line, looking back through a nostalgic haze at this particular place in time.

And it was good, wasn't it, in the face of so many changes—past and impending—to dance. To step out with her freshman roommates in the midst of her last semester. To go shoulder to shoulder with Katie in all their trashy gold and purple glory. The bass dropped as they dipped and rose, writhing and releasing, and in the wash of patterned light that swept over them, they were the goddesses of funkdom, the freaky sisters of soul.

Some weight Rell hadn't even known she was holding began to evaporate; she could practically feel it lifting off. Why had she never danced like this with Trevor? Probably because he only danced to reggae, and there was never any reggae in Crest Top. There were nights she'd gone out dancing with girlfriends, sure, but at some point she'd stopped—probably because she was the one who always wound up trying to keep people from making poor decisions. And yet, looking back, it occurred to Rell that the only poor decision she had ever really made in college was staying with Trevor.

"*Rell*," Katie half whispered, half hissed over her shoulder. "Don't look now."

Rell paused for a moment and then followed Katie's gaze to the door, where a man with a series of piercings down the length of one ear was shooting the breeze with the bouncer.

"Just act natural," she whispered back.

"I'm wearing fake eyelashes and platform boots! How can I act natural?"

The man standing by the door was Alan, the thirty-something-year-old blacksmith who worked sometimes at Rich's Roast, swirling four-leafed clovers into lattes. He lived in a little house down the street from the coffee shop where he'd built a forge in the backyard, twisting iron into fire-breathing dragons and lotus blossoms and the far-out fences that adorned a few of the restaurants downtown. Katie had seen him back there on her way to class, pounding hot metal with a mallet, and now she was in love.

Alan leaned back on the rail, swigging his beer. It wasn't the first time Rell had seen him at Billy Jack's. She remembered one time in particular, the morning after the night before, when she'd returned to the bar to retrieve her card. He'd been standing in virtually that same spot, nursing a beer at ten in the a.m.

"Do you think I should talk to him?" Katie asked.

"Go ahead."

"You hate him!"

"What?"

"Come to the bathroom with me."

But the line for the ladies' stretched clear to the booths at the back of the bar, so they stepped outside onto the back deck instead, shivering in their skimpy outfits. Every time the door opened, competing conversations from the twenty or so women waiting in line spilled toward them, along with the sound of Billy Jack's single women's toilet flushing.

"What do you think?"

The wind shifted, and a gust of wood smoke from the bar's outdoor fireplace momentarily engulfed them. Rell coughed, holding the back of her hand to her mouth. Sifting through her opinions on Katie's various fixations for something halfway diplomatic. "He is, kind of, older."

"He's an artist. He makes these beautiful things, Rell. He has these incredible hands."

"All right, but he seems like kind of a lush."

"You don't know that!"

It was true, Rell didn't know that—maybe the morning after the night before had been a total fluke. Maybe Alan was actually Katie's soul mate. Maybe they'd hit it off tonight, and tomorrow he'd be pounding hot roses just for her. Maybe he was the pot of gold at the end of Katie's personal rainbow, and Rell was just the asshole out there trying to explain how the refraction of light through water vapor sometimes made pretty colors appear in the sky.

Katie was already reapplying her shimmery purple lipstick. "Listen," she said, "I'll see you later."

Back on the dance floor, people were gyrating and gesticulating, rubbing up on each other in one big full-on, funked-out orgy; there was so much sex and perspiration in the air Rell felt the urge to gag. All these people so intent on getting laid—they had no idea what they were headed toward: some lame one-night stand, a lifelong STD, or a deeply dysfunctional relationship that would go on for years.

And Rell, for one, didn't care anymore. She didn't want to be here. Also, she didn't want to be in this stupid outfit, which was probably in some way responsible for her mother getting laid by her dad. She couldn't think of two less compatible people. Probably even she and Trevor had stood a better chance.

And speak of the devil, there they were: Trevor and Trina, cuddled in the corner. Trevor and Trina, bathed in their own special glow. Trina, running her hot little hand over Trevor's dreads. Trevor, smiling at nothing. Was it Rell's imagination, or was he actually *tapping his foot*?

Before they could spot her, she turned away, melting into the line at the bar to close out her tab. She figured Katie would find her way home, but where the hell was Jenna?

Rell spotted Crockett in a pink spandex tank top, and Jenna was right beside him. Two whiskeys on the bar between them, which was not a good sign. Jenna, a Phish fan and therefore a stoner, was not generally known for her tolerance when it came to booze.

"Rell!" Jenna called to her, her adorable little face all flushed. "Look, Crockett dressed up too!"

Crockett's long hair had been pulled back in two French braids, and even his goatee was braided, tied off with the kind of tiny colored rubber bands used by preteen girls to beautify braces. He grinned and leaned toward Rell.

"*What?*" The bass was so loud the wineglasses at the back of the bar were shaking.

He leaned in closer. "I said, can I buy you a drink?"

* * *

That was basically how they wound up at German Jenny's at one in the morning taking shots of tequila. The shots had not been Rell's idea, nor had the German Jen, which was known for its rich douche bags, dolled-up divorcées, and cowboys from the saloon downstairs. But one of those cowboys had offered Crockett three shots of Cuervo to prove his manhood, and Crockett had replied that he was way too much of a pussy to handle three shots by himself. Which everyone seemed to think was hilarious.

"These guys love you," Rell told him. "You should get a horse."

"I have a horse."

"On Sycamore Street?" Crockett, she knew, lived in a crappy little singlewide on a half lot in the barrio. Not exactly the best place for a goat. Hence his habit of walking Molly through the neighborhood on a leash like a dog.

"Back home in Nebraska."

"You're not from Nebraska," Jenna told him. "No one's from Nebraska."

"You're right," Crockett said, a little too loudly. "I'm from California."

"The hell with California," said an old man in a bolo, slamming his fist into the bar. Half of the room cheered. The other half seemed to suddenly find some point of interest in their cell phones.

"What're you having, sir?" Crockett asked.

The old man eyed him unsteadily. This was not the cowboy who'd bought them the shots. This guy looked like he could have been that guy's dad, or granddad, even. "Jameson," he said.

Crockett got the old man's whiskey, and then, for good measure, a round of beers for the bar. "You've got to watch out for those kids from California," Crockett told him. "Especially the ones who walk around in women's clothing."

The old man's watery gaze settled on Crockett's Lion of Judah tattoo, which was peeking up over the bust line of his tank top. Something around the man's mouth twitched. "You go to that school?"

Rell glanced at Jenna. Her roommate was swaying gently, oblivious. Johnny Cash on the jukebox was advising somebody named Bill not to take his guns to town.

"Yes, sir," said Crockett.

"Buncha faggot commie tree-fuckers, if you ask me."

The old man sat as still on his stool as the dummy from the tourist trap downstairs. With his gun in plain view. Why did they live in a state where it was legal to carry firearms in bars? And why were they talking to this guy?

"Are you a fan of gun control, sir?"

If he and Crockett got into it, Rell imagined, this guy would knock him flat on his ass. He was old, but he had that look—like every part of him had already been broken and healed back harder than before.

"Wouldn't say I was," the old man replied.

"I am." Crockett grinned. "Helps with target practice."

The old man did not appear to register this.

"Sir, if you'll excuse us, me and my pinko girlfriends are going to find a spot outside." This drew a couple quiet chuckles from the bar, but the old cowboy just held Crockett's gaze, stone-faced.

Finally, he raised his glass. "Much obliged."

They took a seat at a table on the balcony overlooking Crest Top's courthouse plaza—Jenna first, then Rell, and then Crockett opposite them. Rell leaned across the table and said, "What were you trying to do back there? Start a fight?"

"With that dude? Seriously, he's, like, a hundred years old."

Jenna started laughing, a kind of suppressed snort-gasping punctuated by little pops and squeaks that worked themselves into episodes of open-mouthed, silent hilarity and table-pounding, followed by an almost alarming intake of air. Her roommate was now as drunk as Rell had ever seen her. This was cute, the way almost everything about Jenna was cute, but Crockett didn't even seem to notice.

"I think it's important to push these guys' buttons a little, you know?" He swigged his beer. "If I wasn't ready to take some shit, I wouldn't have come up here dressed like this."

"Oh yeah. I'm sure you put a real dent in the dominant paradigm tonight."

But Crockett was focused elsewhere—specifically, on the big *C* lit up on Crest Top Mountain in the distance. "Back in the day, this town was full of outlaws—Doc Holliday and Billy the Kid, kickin' it. Not to mention some crooked-ass politicians."

"Well, hey," Rell said, "we've still got plenty of those." She knew they were sitting in the German Jen, but at that point, she didn't care. She and everyone she knew had been fighting the Wind Valley Pipeline for years, and by most accounts lost the fight. All the science said that if you pumped the aquifer, you'd kill the river. How the city was just getting away with this was beyond her.

Crockett appeared to be considering her now. "You spent much time on the Greene River?"

The long riparian corridor of the Greene was where Rell had spent her Deep Canyon Wilderness Expedition as a freshman. It was, in fact, where she'd met Trevor, three and a half years previous, along with ten other incoming freshmen.

Other student groups had backpacked the famously photographed wonders of Escalante or Arches or the Grand, but for Rell, nothing would ever compare to floating the Greene River through the red rocks and willows, a lazy tower of cumulus hung overhead.

"You could say that," she told him.

"Have you seen those bulldozers lined up on Goldwater Highway?"

Yes, Rell had seen those bulldozers, stationed beside the turn-off to Wind Valley Road like a line of tanks awaiting orders. They belonged to Blain Contracting, the private part of that unholy public-private partnership hell-bent, as far as she could see, on turning Crest Top into Phoenix.

"They've been sitting there over a month. You know why?"

"Why?"

"Old Man Bonner's suing the city."

"Over what?" The elderly rancher, the patriarch of one of the oldest families in the area, had been working with the Central Arizona Water Alliance to fight the pipeline. The old man had seemed their last, best hope for convincing the ranchers along the pipeline's route not to take Blain's money. But Vern Bonner had failed—everyone knew that.

"Pulled out some old document claiming senior water rights on the Greene. Practically written on parchment paper."

"Will it hold up in court?"

Crockett shrugged. "Probably not. But still."

Now it was Rell's turn to look off into the night. As far as she could tell, the whole town was in bed with Blain Contracting, from the city council on down to Parks and Rec, which had routinely denied them permits to protest the pipeline. And yet, by law, the state had to honor those old claims on its waterways, which would be impossible if the river no longer ran.

Could the lawsuit save the river? After so many years, it seemed too much to hope.

Rell looked back at Crockett, sitting there in his spaghetti straps and pigtails. Trying to ignore the fact that she could see his nipples through the thin pink fabric of his shirt. "How do you know all this? Didn't you just move here?"

Crockett took a pull off his beer. "I've seen it before, in Nebraska. This boomtown outside Omaha passed a safe-yield referendum, just like they did here. All the big developers were pissed because now they had to show how all these crappy tract homes they were building weren't just going to run out of water. Which was pretty much impossible, given the groundwater modeling." He grinned. "Out here, though, it's worse."

Rell cast a glance at Jenna, who was leaning across the table, her head propped up unsteadily in one hand. Rell asked, "What do you mean? Worse how?"

"Half as much rain and twice as many assholes."

Crockett sat there, grinning that shit-eating grin; clearly, he'd said those words before and he'd say them again. And maybe he was right about the rainfall—when Rell thought about it, he probably was—but she wondered, what did he know about Arizona? Crockett had come in with Katie's class. He'd lived here all of two months. "I didn't realize this state had cornered the market on assholes."

"Are you kidding? These people beat the Apaches."

These were lines, set pieces, complete with beats. Still, Rell couldn't help but laugh a bit at that. And had this boy really just dropped the term *groundwater modeling* in the course of casual conversation? Despite herself, she could feel the hard shell that had grown around her geeky heart starting to dissolve in his presence.

Crockett leaned closer. "But you know something amazing? When you pour concrete mortar in the fuel pump of a bulldozer, it *dramatically* decreases that bulldozer's environmental impact."

Rell just shook her head. Thinking, *This boy is fucking with me, just like he was fucking with that old cowboy at the bar.*

"You're so full of shit." Jenna had lain down across her outstretched arm. "Crockett, why are you always so full of shit?"

But Crockett wasn't looking at Jenna. Crockett was looking at Rell. "You have any idea how much one of those big hydraulic excavators goes for?" he asked. And, when she failed to respond: "A hundred thou, easy." He licked his bottom lip. "It'd be a shame if a few of those bad boys wound up out of commission tonight."

Through the door to the bar inside, a woman laughed. The jukebox was playing Top 40 country now, and a slick steel-guitar riff drifted toward them.

"You know," Rell said, "you should careful, propositioning girls like that."

Crockett lifted an eyebrow. His knee was touching hers now under the table. "I'm not scared."

She could feel his gaze on her body, like a breeze, felt it riffle over the bare skin of her arms. How long had it been since a man looked at her like that? The night had turned cold, which only served to accentuate the warmth where their bodies were touching, the promise of heat his body held.

In his dark brown eyes, she could see the rest of the night unfolding: they would drop Jenna off at home and then drive out Goldwater Highway, sitting close in the cab of his truck. Because, of course, he owned a truck. And of course she would go with him on this night raid, this counterattack, such as the Apaches might have conducted. Rell wanted this, suddenly. To let that spark of anger in her, kindled over the course of so many drawn-out city council meetings, so many pointless petitions and protests, catch hold of some tinder and burn. She wanted to laugh with Crockett while they funneled mortar into the tanks of those offensive excavators, high on adrenaline, and kiss long and deep, breathless. She wanted to sleep with him in the desert tonight, just like that song her mom had always so cheesily loved.

Just for once, she wanted to do this wild, indefensible thing. To say later she'd been drunk on tequila, that it had seemed like a good idea at the time.

But here at last was the sad truth of Rell's sensible existence: She *was* drunk on tequila—drunk to the point where she knew she'd be leaving the Vulva downtown and calling a cab. Drunk to the point where she would require Crockett's assistance to get Jenna off of this table and into its backseat. Drunk enough that she might just pass out in her gold lamé super bells, a stiff cloud of metallic hairspray stuck in her hair, rather than bothering to shower and change. But even so, it didn't seem like a good idea.

* * *

If Rell had taken Crockett up on his offer that night, she probably would have woken up the next morning and regretted that she had. As it was, she woke up and regretted that she hadn't.

At least she'd managed to get herself into pajamas before passing out. Big win there. She should have been proud. Proud she wasn't waking up naked next to someone she'd met a total of two times. Proud she hadn't contracted herpes or genital warts or something possibly worse that had yet even to be named. Proud that she hadn't committed any felonies, any crimes of passion or property.

But waking up alone on a Sunday morning and walking downstairs to find the sink full of dirty dishes, Rell felt more depressed than she had at any point since the breakup.

Katie had covered the stovetop in crusted blotches of tomato soup. Jenna had left not only her and Scott's dishes but also four paper towels full of sprouted seeds, now dried out crisp on the counter. Rell pulled the paper apart; most of the sprouts were dead, but a few were still doing their best to unfurl their hard little leaves.

She dug dirt from the backyard, filled an egg tray, and then carefully planted and watered each of the surviving sprouts. Of course, the garden beds had never been finished, so she spent the next hour or so breaking up and turning over dirt, working in steer manure from the bags Scott had helped them pile up by the shed. Which reminded her that Katie hadn't turned over the compost the way she'd promised to, so Rell spent a while on that too, digging down deep into the layers of dry leaves, newspaper, and desiccated kitchen scraps. Wondering, in sort of an abstract way, what her problem was.

She'd wanted to say yes to Crockett the night before. She'd wanted to be Doc to his Billy the Kid, sticking it to the crooked politicians. Which, granted, probably would have been a poor decision. But she was still young enough for poor decisions, wasn't she?

Rell looked up to find a goat in the garden: Molly. She stood by the fence that bordered the alley, pulling at the horehound, as natural as you please. As if she were some free-ranging denizen of the barrio—a raccoon, maybe, or one of those feral cats that trolled the local bird-feeders with the workaday regularity of commercial fishermen.

The goat lifted her head and fixed Rell with one blue eye. It seemed for a moment as if this mysterious creature was trying to tell her something. About her own essential animal nature, maybe.

In retrospect, Rell would say, it seemed a sign. Though at that point, it's possible she was just tired of making sense. This goat, in this neighborhood, did not make sense. It didn't need to make sense.

It was a fucking goat, was it not? It was what it was.

* * *

Crockett's dinged-up singlewide sat on a half lot behind an outcropping of boulders toward the end of Sycamore Street. It was one of those places you might not notice, walking by, but just up the drive, the place was a bustling center of barnyard activity: chickens scattered as Rell and Molly ambled past a makeshift coop and pen, where a potbellied pig was snuffling up kitchen scraps.

Actually, no—that was a javelina. It seemed the chickens ranged free here on Crockett's sustainable urban homestead, scrounging up bugs from the gravel, graciously leaving their feed for the wild pigs of the desert to dine on. These pigs (which weren't pigs at all, but a kind of peccary) possessed poor eyesight but a keen sense of smell; as soon as the javelina got wind of Molly and Rell, it bolted through the open gate and back up into the boulders beside the trailer.

She knocked on the door with one hand, the old climbing rope she'd tied around the goat's neck in the other. No reply. There was a truck (of course) parked in the drive, but that didn't mean anything, necessarily; Crockett, like most Deep Canyon students, in his commitment to the low-carbon lifestyle, relied primarily on his bike. Which was possibly that red Cannondale leaning on the fence, which seemed familiar—a girl's model, but she didn't imagine he'd mind.

Rell knocked on the door again and took a step back. For a moment she considered just shutting Molly back in her pen and walking away. Then she heard the sound of a drawer opening inside the trailer; something crashed and someone swore. The door swung open and there stood Crockett, his hair frizzed out from his braids the night before, looking not in the least bit sexy in his boxers and bathrobe.

"Hey," he said.

"Your goat," Rell said, feeling lame.

Crockett looked down at Molly. As if surprised to discover that he did, in fact, own a goat. He looked like maybe he had gone three rounds with that old cowboy the night before. Plus, his breath could have knocked over a horse.

He invited her in, offered her a seat on what appeared to be the only clear surface in the living room—a hard-backed chair with half its caning caved in—and then excused himself to the kitchen. (But not before, she noticed, discreetly palming a condom wrapper off the couch.)

Crockett's little living room was carpeted in orange shag and decorated with reggae posters. He had all the classics—Bob Marley, Jimmy Cliff, Bunny Wailer—as well as Midnite, whom he was apparently a big fan of, just like Rell's ex. And just like her ex, Crockett had a hand-blown glass bong in the shape of a dragon proudly displayed atop his bookshelf, like a priceless Ming vase. Which seemed fitting, considering.

To his credit, Crockett had fresh coffee beans—she watched from the living room as he pulled a bag from the freezer and ground them before setting the coffeemaker to perk. To his further credit, he was apparently aware of his breath; she could hear him brushing his teeth at the kitchen sink.

"Goat milk all right?" he asked.

"Sure."

"It's not the best place for a goat," he said, conversationally. "But I'm lactose intolerant, and goat milk is crazy expensive."

"Makes sense," she said, though it didn't, really, unless he had a two-quart-a-day habit.

And then Crockett was beside her with two mugs in one hand, sweeping the coffee table clear with the other. Two empty forties dropped to the shag, spilling their stale remains; Rell couldn't help it. She wrinkled her nose.

"Sorry about the mess." Crockett settled on the arm of the couch beside her. "I had some people over last night."

Rell cast a glance at an empty pizza box on the floor. Like the paper plate and the crust beside it, that box had clearly occupied the same position for weeks.

"You get some sleep?"

"Oh yeah," she said, "sleep. It's what I do best."

He leaned closer, as if confiding a secret. "I had some crazy dreams last night."

And it was amazing, really: She would sooner have eaten scrambled eggs off that manky shag than consented to take her clothes off amid such squalor. But it seemed suddenly possible that Crockett might kiss her and she might let him.

She heard a soft cough from the bedroom. A girl's cough, followed by a groan—the kind that generally accompanies a monstrous hangover. Rell felt her face go still. Hadn't she seen a girl's bike out there by the fence?

How had it not occurred to her that Jenna might have ridden over to Crockett's that morning?

Rell took a long pull of her coffee. The only way out of this was to leave. Immediately. In the same moment, however, she realized that her butt had actually wedged itself into the hole in her chair. Getting out would require leaning over, ridiculously, to set the mug on the table and then grasping the seat with both hands and hoisting her ass aloft.

Rell took another swig of coffee, marshaling her resources, but just then the bedroom door creaked open.

Standing there in her clothes from the night before was Katie, one purple eyelash clinging haphazardly to her face. "Oh, hey," she said.

"Rell brought back Molly," Crockett offered, by way of explanation.

"Cool," said Katie. "You got his goat."

"Hey," Rell said, before she could stop herself, "looks like you got it first."

"Care for coffee, Kate?" Crockett asked. "I've got some on."

"Yeah," said Rell. "He got it on. For me earlier, but now for you too." *Shut up, shut up, shut up,* she told herself. She sat her cup down, got her ass out of the seat, and stood. Crockett stood too, like a game of musical chairs.

"You're leaving?" he said. "You just got here."

Rell looked over at Katie. Who was clearly too embarrassed now to meet her eye. Why? Did she think Rell was going to judge her? Deliver some lecture, perhaps, on the evils of collegiate promiscuity?

Why so uptight? Bob Marley, holding a spliff, seemed to ask her. *Why not stay awhile?*

"Yeah," Rell said, sitting her ass back down. "Whatever. I just got here."

So they spent the next twenty minutes or so beneath the benevolent gaze of Bob, swilling coffee with Crockett. He regaled them with tales of his hardscrabble youth, growing up outside Audacious, Nebraska. He claimed his father was a truck farmer, the last of the breed. With whom he'd fallen out of favor when he went punk rock in Omaha.

"How'd you get here?" Rell asked. "To Deep Canyon?"

"This buddy of mine."

"No," she said, "I mean, how'd you swing it financially?" Tuition at their school was notoriously steep. She'd had to take both an early-morning shift at the bagel shop and an afternoon work-study gig to cover the shortfall in her loans. Crockett, she knew, pulled a shift here and there in the school's bike shop with Jenna, but he had to have blown more on booze last night at the German Jen than he made doing that in a week.

"Scholarships," Crockett said. And then, after a moment's modesty: "I did all right in school."

Did the bong come with the scholarship? Rell wanted to ask him. Because as far as she knew, Deep Canyon College didn't offer anything approaching a full ride unless you were a 78-percent registered Native American war veteran in a wheelchair.

Crockett placed his hand on her knee. And the other, outrageously, on Katie's. "So," he said, apropos of nothing, "would you like to see the rest of the house?" It was suddenly so clear what he had in mind that Rell almost laughed out loud.

Maybe she *was* uptight, the way Trevor had always alleged. Maybe she was, in fact, the biggest prude on the face of the earth. But she was also way too old for this sort of shit.

"Actually," Rell said, "I better hit it."

* * *

They walked home in silence.

"You were right," Katie said, finally, "about Alan. He was pretty much plastered last night. And Crockett—he's such a sweet guy. He walked me home, and we stayed up talking."

Talking. Rell shook her head. Like somebody's mother, maybe.

"Anyway, I hope Jenna's not all pissed. At least now it'll be easier for her."

Rell cast her a glance.

"With Scott."

Once again, Rell found herself amazed by Katie's ability to rationalize—the way she could make herself believe, really *believe*, just about anything.

"I just want you to know." Katie covered her mouth and gave a little cough. "This is different."

"Different how?"

"Just—" Katie sniffed the air. "Different. From those other guys. Like Alan." She looked up. "You smell that?"

Rell caught a whiff of it then, the sharp tang of wood smoke. "It's a control burn."

"A what?"

"A control burn. The Forest Service sets the woods on fire this time of year, while there's still some moisture left over from the winter. To keep it from going up later."

Katie squinted. "Why not just let nature do its thing?"

Here Rell really had no choice but to stop in the middle of the street. "Do you even understand what you're saying? That would mean letting this whole town burn down this summer."

Katie just shrugged, like that was no big deal, and kept walking.

Rell was seized by the need to explain. How fires in the National Forest had been repressed for a hundred years, resulting in woodlands choked with bone-dry brush at the edge of town, where all the new developments were. About the drought, the lightning, the three months remaining until the monsoons broke, *if* they broke. Last summer's storms had brought more wind than rain, and wind fueled fire; all it took was a spark.

Rell wanted to express all this to Katie, to use the right words, to speak them clearly—to impress upon her the importance of defensible space. Fuel breaks. Boundaries.

But Katie was smiling to herself in a personal way now, walking away down the street. Smiling in the way of fools and fanatics. Katie, the girl in the trashy tube top with a rainbow in her heart.

Two

Drylands Ecology

RELL SAT AT THE KITCHEN TABLE with the Arizona high country laid out before her.

To the right of her laptop lay the yellowing map that picked out the state's elevation in fine successive whorls, like ripples on the sea floor, from the Colorado Plateau south to the Mogollon Rim, that line through the middle of the state that divided it nearly in two, the highlands from the hotlands, the blizzards of Flagstaff from the inferno of Phoenix. To her left lay a topographic map of Bridal Creek, its stippled green print revealing every twist, ridge, and rise of the northern Bradshaw Mountains, stitched through with fine threads of blue.

Rell had other maps folded away—maps that showed the proposed route of the pipeline, from Crest Top north to Wind Valley, through the ranches that Blain Contracting had bought out or was attempting to intimidate as of the previous fall. All of those ranches had since acquiesced, which meant there was nothing stopping the city now from laying the pipe that would pump the Wind Valley aquifer dry but one very old man and his very old water rights claim, which no one at city hall had any record of because it hailed from before Crest Top was a city.

Those maps had nothing to do with Rell's senior thesis, tentatively entitled *Fire on the Mountain: Seed Morphology in the Bridal Creek Watershed.* And yet, looking at these maps, she kept seeing the others—the maps that would change this landscape forever.

The author Mary Austin, like the Native Americans she'd admired, had called the Southwest "land of little rain." And yet, Rell thought, what little it received defined it. Every ripple of elevation on those maps, every crease and crenellation, sought to call down the rain from the clouds as they passed on their urgent business from the Pacific east to Corpus Christi. In the desert you could read your altitude in the trees, or the absence thereof: ponderosas and Doug firs up high, juniper and pinyon in the midranges, and chaparral and creosote in the lowlands, sparsely spaced.

From the road, springs and creeks were visible as ribbons of green in an otherwise dry landscape. Up close, they revealed a riot of wildlife, from songbirds to salamanders, fish to frogs. Those oases supported greater species diversity in a few hundred feet than many landscapes supported in a few hundred miles.

Most of the state was minimally populated, but wherever water was, or had been, a town had bloomed, often in the footprint of its ghost: Phoenix had been founded upon the ancient irrigation ditches of the Hohokam, and the city of Greene River on what had, during the Late Middle Ages, been a bustling metropolis of the Anasazi.

The Anasazi and Hohokam people had disappeared long before the white settlers arrived—long before the Hopi and Navajo, even. No one knew why, but various theories indicated "unsustainable resource use" combined with drought. Rell could not help but reflect on that whenever she passed one of those old roads around Crest Top—White Springs and Burnt Springs and Yavapai Creek Canyon—that referred to features of the landscape that no longer existed. The region's water table had been dropping precipitously since the 1960s, and not one of the creeks that had led to the founding of Crest Top still ran year round. Some, like the Bridal, had been reduced to arroyos, ditches through which the forest threw off the violent cloudbursts of the monsoons. Even the mighty Colorado River, which had carved the Grand Canyon, no longer reached the sea.

And still people like George Blain were intent on draining this place and paving it, on bulldozing and building it up, on sucking every last drop of water from this fine, fragile landscape and its unique biota in favor of rich retirees in McMansions. As if Crest Top was not surrounded on three sides by a tinderbox of National Forest seasoned by three years of drought.

As if the greatest drought of them all was not yet to come.

Rell picked up a photograph from the stack she'd checked out of the local historical museum, which she'd piled up beside her laptop. The photo was an aerial from the Angus Mountain fire of '78; the burn stopped at the Greene River, sparing the city that bore its name. She shuffled through the stack until she found a similar aerial, taken in 1996. The burn site was barely visible, but the ribbon of green that indicated the river's path had shrunk.

What would happen when that river was no longer there?

Rell looked up to find Katie rooting around in the cupboard by the sink.

"Hey," Rell said. It was the first she had seen of Katie in some time—maybe a week. "You spend the night at Crockett's?"

"No." Katie poured herself a cup from the Mr. Coffee by the stove. "At the Cat. Getting ready for the protest."

"What protest?"

"The pipeline protest."

Rell glanced at her laptop. Though the clock read ten fifteen, the cursor was still sitting in the same paragraph she'd been working and reworking since six, when Katie had no doubt been deep in the late stages of REM. "What's happening with the pipeline? I thought it was on hold until the lawsuit was settled."

"That's why the protest is at the courthouse."

"You think showing up there is going to sway the judge?"

Katie walked over to the table and sat her cup of coffee down—on the corner, Rell noticed, of the historical museum's photograph. "It's not about that."

Rell slid the photo out from under Katie's mug. "What's it about, then?"

Katie swung a chair around so she was sitting facing Rell with her legs to either side of its back, which was upholstered in a kitschy psychedelic vinyl Rell had hated on sight. Leave it to Katie to pick that chair from the entire mismatched set from which to launch her offensive.

"Have you heard?" she asked. "About the Bonner Ranch?"

No, Rell had not heard about the Bonner Ranch. Beyond work and school, pretty much all of her waking hours had been focused on this same collection of maps and photographs for the better part of a month.

"Somebody set off dynamite around one of Vern Bonner's cow tanks. It started a fire."

"When?"

"Yesterday." Katie scratched at a mark on the back of the chair where the vinyl had peeled back, probably from a burn. "With dynamite from Blain. They're reporting it as stolen."

"Of course they are."

"The police say they're trying to find a man who fits the description George Blain gave them."

"George Jr., maybe? In a ski mask? Maybe a Deep Canyon hoodie?"

Katie just fixed her with that sorrowful, almost unbearably sincere look she seemed to have perfected lately. As if humor were a planet in a galaxy far, far away.

"Hey," Rell said, "maybe you should be protesting the cop shop instead." It was intended as a joke—really, nothing about

Crest Top surprised her anymore—but it came out more like a gibe. She tried again. "You said the explosions started a fire?"

Katie nodded, taking a cautious sip of her coffee, though whatever she'd found in the pot hadn't been hot in over an hour.

Out of the corner of her eye, Rell saw something skitter across the countertop. She blinked. Maybe she'd just imagined it. "How far did it spread? Is it still burning?"

Katie shrugged. Such details were beyond her.

Rell tapped the words *Bonner Ranch fire* into her browser, and there it was on the website of the local daily, in an article with a time stamp from yesterday morning: *Explosives Damage Property, Kill Livestock—Firefighters are working to contain the fires sparked by the explosions....* And then another, from later that day: *Bonner Ranch Burning.* An update had the fire eight miles east of Wind Valley Road, encompassing 30 acres, 20 percent contained, with prevailing winds out of the east. "At least the fire's on the west side of the ranch."

Katie's ash-brown eyebrows twitched, as if she was suspicious of such facts. "What difference does that make?"

"It's all grasslands around there. With a wind out of the east, the fire will just burn toward the road, and that'll act as a fuel break."

Katie's expression was blank.

"Fuel breaks stop fires," Rell explained. "Fires need fuel to keep burning."

Katie licked her bottom lip. "Everyone knows it's George Blain trying to get Bonner to drop the lawsuit, but the police aren't even investigating him."

Again, Rell caught the movement out of the corner of her eye—it was, undeniably, a mouse, scurrying behind that old plastic coffeemaker they kept duct-taping back together. Emboldened, no doubt, by the reused bulk bag of granola with the hole in the bottom that Katie had pulled out of the cupboard, spilling its crunchy contents across the counter. Rell opened her mouth to say something but then thought better of it. If she did, she would be the one who would have to do something about it. Better just to pretend that mouse wasn't sitting there on the counter behind the coffeemaker, waiting for them to leave. Rell would be moving out soon anyway. Let Katie and Jenna debate the ethical implications of live traps versus dead ones. Let them deal with the grown-up business.

Let them put out these fires.

Katie sat her cup back on the table—far too close, this time, to Rell's laptop. She said, "The protest is at three tomorrow."

"Don't you have your seminar tomorrow?"

"You should come."

Rell moved Katie's coffee cup to the left. "You know, I don't think I can make it." She kept her gaze trained on her computer screen, but even so, she could feel the way Katie was looking at her over the top of that chair, judging her.

Rell was glad that her freshman roommate had taken up the cause. Really, she was; fighting the Wind Valley Pipeline would give Katie real-world experience with the sorts of environmental issues she'd be learning about in class, the same way it had for Rell—the same way she had claimed on all those job applications she'd sent out that spring. And yet, the way Katie was staring at her now, the way she'd cornered her here in the kitchen while she was trying to work, was really just sort of irritating in the extreme.

Eventually—after a period of awkward silence longer than virtually anyone else would have endured—Katie said, "Do you mind my asking why not?"

"I'm way behind on my paper." Rell did her best to keep her tone even.

"How is that even possible? You've been working so hard on it." The fact that Katie was trying to be nice made it sound even bitchier.

"Your senior thesis is a big deal, all right? You'll see when you get there." Which, in turn, came out bitchier than Rell had intended. "Plus, I have to work."

"You could call off."

Sure, Rell could call off. While she was at it, why not get an extension on her thesis? She could go on to not graduate and pay for an extra semester with money she didn't have, while Katie here pissed away her parents' prodigious piles of cash by skipping classes and marching around the Crest Top County Courthouse Plaza with all those pretty puppets she'd made, chanting slogans. Like that was going to stop the kind of people who responded to a lawsuit by blowing up a man's cow tanks.

"Katie, you got here six months ago. This has been going on for six years."

"That's not fair."

Finally, Rell looked up at her. "You know what's not fair? This fucking conversation."

"Look, I'm sorry." Katie's big brown eyes, her best feature, were soft. "But Rell—"

"This is the only place in the house with enough room for me to work. It's not okay for you to just—"

"When you look back, don't you want to know you did everything you could?"

Rell leaned forward at the table. So many thoughts were running through her head, and so few seemed likely to make any dent whatsoever in the bubble currently surrounding Katie's. Like, where did she get off, pressuring Rell like this—after all the petitions she had circulated, all the times she'd stood up to speak in city council, all the protests she herself had attended? And what made Katie think it was okay to approach her like this, in the final few hours she had to turn an entire semester's worth of work into something vaguely intelligible? "You know, this might be hard for you to understand right now—"

Katie opened her mouth; Rell held up her hand.

"But if there's one thing I've learned, living here, it's that the desert is not a nice place. Beautiful, but not nice. Really, it's kind of a bitch." Rell held her gaze. "It'll suck you dry if you let it."

"Listen." Katie's voice was soft. "I know you and a lot of people have been pushing on this for a long time. And I know you're graduating soon."

Not soon enough, Rell couldn't help but think.

"But we can't stop now."

Rell let her eyes drift shut for a moment. "Katie," she said quietly. "For fuck's sake."

Her roommate stood. "It's two hours out of your day."

Rell just shook her head as Katie walked away. Because Katie was right, wasn't she? It was two hours out of her day.

There was just no way to say the truth, which was that Rell was done fighting. This place had broken her heart.

* * *

That day at work she left the bagels in the oven too long, reducing an entire batch of Asiago to blackened hockey pucks. She put roast beef on somebody's veggie sandwich and chili sauce on a PB&J—and in the latter case, actually made a small child cry. That conversation with Katie kept replaying in her head, and every time it did—*It's two hours out of your day*—Rell found herself arguing with Katie, defending herself, rehearsing for a rematch.

Why? she wondered. Why did it bother her so much? Sure, Katie was earnest, but what freshman at Deep Canyon College for the Liberal Arts and the Environment was not earnest? At Katie's age, Rell had earnestly believed all sorts of stupid things.

For instance, what Joseph Campbell had said: *Follow your bliss, and doors will open where there were no doors before.* Like Katie, Rell had followed her bliss out West. She'd followed her bliss down rivers, up mountains, and through luminous red-rock canyons. She'd followed her bliss into a senior thesis that rivaled a graduate thesis, which had been written up in such geeky publications as *Western Wildfire Quarterly.* And yet, working the lunch rush at the bagel shop on a Tuesday, the same way she had for the last three years, Rell could not help but feel acutely aware of the fact that she'd followed her bliss into forty thousand dollars worth of debt, and out of no less than thirty job applications, sent out to what seemed like every environmental nonprofit west of the Mississippi, not a single door had opened.

When the rush slowed to a trickle, Rell's coworker cut her loose and she stepped out under the awning to roll herself a smoke. It was the fussy sort of green-and-white striped awning favored by those shotgun shops with pressed-tin ceilings lined up down Ransom Row—so named, according to legend, because a couple of ruffians had once held a local madam hostage in a back room of the Silver Spur until their bar tab had been paid by her patrons. It was the sort of questionably historical drama reenacted by costumed old ladies and gents from the Gardner Museum for the benefit of the same tourists who kept Tombstone in business.

Next door, the lady from the candy shop was futzing with her flowers, a collection of purple pansies clustered around a sign: *We Support Our Troops.* Nearly every establishment on the row besides Flip's and Billy Jack's had posted something similar somewhere: a yellow ribbon in the window, *I Stand with the President* on the mirror at the back of the bar, a wanted poster, Old West style, with Osama bin Laden's mild face emblazoned on it. It was one of the things Rell would miss least about this place when she left it—the knee-jerk jingoism, the rah-rah patriotism, the gleeful way people here had embraced the war, as if it were some high-stakes sporting event.

The lady from next door lifted one penciled-on eyebrow in Rell's direction. Did she disapprove, perhaps, of the way Rell was eyeing her sign? Did she find Rell's expression insufficiently enthusiastic? Or was the old gal perchance under the impression that she was out here on the sidewalk rolling herself a jay?

"What up, Rell."

"What up, Arin."

Arin was a pretty little brown-skinned punk with a shaved head, a townie, who worked at the bakery next door. They'd met at a pipeline protest a few years back and talked maybe once or twice at the coffee shop, but they'd never done more than lift a hand in passing at work. "What are you doing out here?" Rell asked her.

"Taking a smoke break."

"Since when do you smoke?" As far as Rell knew, Arin was vegan and straight-edge and had the pink, blushing lungs of a nun.

"I don't. But think about it." Arin leaned back against the old red bricks of Ransom Row. "How many times per shift do you come out here to smoke?"

Rell measured out tobacco from her pouch. "I don't know. Maybe twice?"

"You probably spend five or ten minutes out here each time. That's ten or twenty minutes of break time people who don't smoke don't get. Plus, you have an excuse to go outside."

Rell looked down at her cigarette. "You're right," she said. "I should quit."

"Why?"

"It just seems irresponsible, considering."

"Quit if you want to quit. I'm not trying to make you feel bad. I just saw you out here and thought, you know what? Fuck it. I'm going out there too." Arin cast her a sidelong glance. "Unless you'd rather be alone."

"No, I didn't mean it like that." The way Rell said it came off as defensive, which wasn't the way she'd intended it. What she should have said was, *No, it's cool*, the same straightforward way Arin would have said it—like it was a statement of fact, not a tail-wagging competition. It wasn't that Arin came off in a way that was masculine, exactly, despite that newsboy cap and those heavy black combat boots. It was more that she came across in a way that was generally neutral, which was maybe not something Rell had ever seen in a woman, especially a young woman. Like she was responsible for herself, completely, but not necessarily for anyone else.

"Arin, can I ask you something?"

"Shoot."

"How old are you?"

"Nineteen."

Rell lit her cigarette and took a drag, letting it out slowly. "That's what I thought."

"Why?"

"You just seem a lot more mature than my roommates."

Arin chuckled, a dry sound. "You go to Deep Canyon, don't you?"

"Yes," Rell said, "I go to Deep Canyon. In fact, I'm about to graduate from Deep Canyon. And it's a good thing too, because I'm not sure how much longer I can handle my current living arrangement."

"Weren't you out in Bridal Creek?"

"I was. But then my ex left me for this hot rock-climber chick. Turns out, he'd been screwing her behind my back for months."

"That's cold."

Rell opened her mouth to take issue with that—to explain how Trevor just wasn't all that good at communicating, especially in situations involving potential conflict—but then stopped herself. Why, after everything, did she still have the urge to defend him? Arin was right. What Trevor had done was cold. As cold as the foot of snow he'd made her shovel that day, alone, just to get her car out of his driveway. Like, really? After everything they'd been through, everything they'd shared, he couldn't have done that much for her? She pulled on her cigarette, feeling the nicotine hit her bloodstream, and laughed sort of a humorless laugh that made her sound, she imagined, like she was fifty years old, hot on the heels of her second divorce. "Now I'm living in this funky old house in the barrio with the most atrocious linoleum this side of 1974. It's so drafty that sometimes the curtains move when the windows are shut. And it's like no one ever cleans the place besides me. Today I caught a mouse munching granola on our kitchen counter." Rell took another drag, mostly for effect. "One of my roommates is in this relationship that's obviously going nowhere, but she won't break up with the guy. It's like she'd rather cheat on him than tell him to his face."

Arin had thick, dark eyebrows, and when she raised them like that, it made the gesture seem more pointed than it would have on someone else. Rell looked off.

"And my other roommate—I don't know. She's this sort of preppy girl from Connecticut or something who's suddenly decided she's an activist."

"I know who you're talking about. Kathy something?"

"Katie Callahan."

"Boat shoes? Salon blond? Wears that little mushroom on a hemp necklace?"

"That's the one."

Arin nodded. "She hangs out a lot at the Cat."

It made sense that Arin would know Katie, as the Black Cat was where all the local punk bands played. "Right," Rell said, "and because she hangs out at the Cat, she's decided it's more important for me to go to this pipeline protest tomorrow than it is to finish my senior thesis. Even though I've spent the last three years protesting the Wind Valley Pipeline, and now I've got, like, a week to finish this fifty-page paper, and I work two jobs." Rell directed a stream of smoke up at the awning. "Where does she get off?"

Arin nodded, but she didn't look as sympathetic as Rell would have liked.

"I mean, is my going or not going to this protest really going to change anything?"

"Probably not." Arin took a step toward the street, out of Rell's stream of carcinogens. "But that's not why you're pissed."

"Oh yeah? Why am I pissed?"

Arin studied her, as if gauging how much to say. "You're pissed because you're this working-class sort of hippie chick who probably spends a half hour trying to decide which type of organic toilet paper to buy, even though you can barely pay your rent. And Katie is this dumb little East Coast freshman with a two-hundred-dollar dye job who gets her shirts at the Gap. And—" Arin stopped.

"What?"

"She's trying to shame you as a liberal."

"Well, hell," Rell said, and they both laughed, because obviously it was true. When Arin smiled like that, really smiled, it showed off her high cheekbones, her dark eyes. When Arin smiled, Rell found, it was best to look elsewhere. Like across the street, at the behemoth trucks parked the length of Ransom Row—and beyond them, at the Crest Top County Courthouse, where Vern Bonner's water rights claim would be decided that summer, in June.

Not that the outcome mattered, really; Rell would be gone by then.

Finally, she said, "It's just the same handful of baby boomers and students at every protest, the same funky families and their little kids. The same blowhard old man in socks and Birkenstocks—"

"Oh yeah. What's his name?"

"—giving the same speech to the same people. And nobody will cut him off, because no one wants to be the bad guy, even though—"

"He's a blowhard and everyone knows it."

"And what about the dude who thinks he's from the Pleiades?"

"The one who always wears the Area 51 trucker hat?"

"He's in every picture." Rell took a drag from her cigarette and coughed. "Like, is he really helping the cause?"

Arin folded her arms and looked off. In that black cap, gray T-shirt, and white apron, she could have been a clerk from the dry goods store that the bagel shop and bakery once were. Was she gay? Was she not? Rell couldn't quite tell. One way or another, Arin would never appear in a Chamber of Commerce ad for Crest Top, Arizona. And yet she looked right there, standing beneath that striped green awning, against those old red bricks. She fit.

"Seriously." Arin spat on the warm pavement. "It's a shame."

"What's a shame?"

"More people don't give a shit."

* * *

As Rell set off on her bike ride home, she thought about that. Though the grassroots resistance to the Wind Valley Pipeline had been vocal, what Arin had said was true: it had always been small. Maybe because so many people had moved to Crest Top to retire—so they could, in fact, cease to give a shit. Maybe because the resistance was based in part out of Deep Canyon College, and students were always packing up and moving on. Or maybe George Blain and his cronies had ruled this town for so long that no one even bothered to oppose him anymore.

She rode her mountain bike down the alley behind the bars and shops and restaurants of Ransom Row, where a Hispanic fry-cook stood smoking in his hairnet—right down Hall and left on Geronimo, where caution was required: a third of the drivers in this town were over the age of sixty and either did not see well or did not care to. At the light Rell hopped her bike up onto the sidewalk and crossed at the crosswalk to the other side of the street—where, at the intersection of Geronimo and Powell, the wooded expanse of Quartz Creek loomed off to the left.

The entrance to the bike trail didn't look like much, just a mosaic-decorated trash can made by some local schoolkids and the horseshoe pits off to one side. But beyond those minor landmarks lay a hard-packed path that swept down into the green-gold kingdom of the cottonwoods, tweeting and cheeping with birds.

Rell rolled under the old railroad trestle and over the bridge. The creek was just a few pools of single-celled sludge at this time of year, but the roots of the trees pulled from the moisture deep below, creating pockets of cool air in the warming day, like fleeting thoughts through which she flew.

Once again, Rell found herself thinking about the Greene River, the great green muscle of it pushing south to the Salt. How much was the temperature of the entire state affected by that huge evaporative cooler? And how many birds depended on it, that oasis spanning nearly two hundred miles, in the course of their migrations from Central America to Canada, through that long, dry stretch of the Pacific Flyway that extended from the deserts of Sonora to the foothills of the Rockies?

Rell put on speed, circling Quartz Creek Park with the wind in her hair, and then slowed as she hit the next leg of the trail, which was filled with lanky young trees sporting white plastic socks, cordoned off with caution tape. A sign announced that this area was being restored with native plants, courtesy of the Central Arizona Water Alliance. Rell had helped to plant those trees as part of a block class, and though the area still looked pretty hit up—not long ago, it had been the barrio's unofficial dump—every time she passed it, she imagined the way it would look when all those willows and sycamores grew tall and broad and formed a cool kingdom of their own.

Then she was rolling past the back of those old miner's shacks at the end of Second Street. There was the sculpture someone seemed to be coaxing from the stump of an old cottonwood that had fallen that winter, and there was the Black Cat. Rell stood up in her stirrups, leaned left, and exited the bike trail at top speed, racing into the wind. As much as she'd loved the mountain bike trails in the Bradshaws where she'd lived with Trevor, there was something exhilarating about a trail like this, which ran right through the heart of town, unseen. Life at 737 Sycamore Street might have had its complaints, but her commute to work was not one of them.

A black Audi with California plates sat ticking in the driveway. Rell pushed in through the front door to the hall and found Katie in the kitchen, sitting across the table from an extremely fit fiftyish woman with a blond bob. She rose as Rell entered the room. "You must be Rell," she said, extending her hand.

"And you must be Katie's mom." So here was Sandra Callahan, the senator from—where was it again? Rhode Island? Delaware? One of the small states. Her hand felt cool to the touch.

"Mom was speaking at a conference in Phoenix," Katie explained, in a slightly odd tone. "She decided to stop by."

Her mother laughed, as if that were a joke. "I couldn't come all the way out here and not see my girl."

Which seemed perfectly reasonable to Rell, but it was clear from the look on Katie's face—her whole bearing, really—that she considered this surprise visit the height of embarrassment.

"How long are you in town for?" Rell asked, ostensibly to be polite. In reality, she was wondering how long it would be until these two relinquished the table so she could work.

"Oh, I'll be flying out yet tonight." Again, Katie's mom laughed. Exactly the way she had before. "I just wanted to see how Katie was doing this semester. And to meet the new roommate! Well, not exactly new anymore." She settled her full attention upon Rell, and now Rell could feel the full intensity of it, the way this woman smiled. Like stage makeup, it might seem natural from far away, but up close, it seemed exaggerated, extreme. "Tell me, Rell, what's your major?"

"Environmental science. I'll graduate with a dual competence in drylands ecology and native plant conservation."

Sandra looked at Katie, even as she spoke to Rell. "Would you say that was a practical major? In terms of employment?"

"Oh yeah. Super employable."

Katie's mother missed the irony, the suggestion that Rell had recently come to reevaluate just how employable this major was. She was still smiling at Katie, beaming that campaign-train smile.

In her flattest voice, Katie said, "Mom found out I switched my major."

"To what?"

"Arts and letters."

"I thought it was arts and letters."

Katie cast a glance at her mom. "Not originally."

Sandra put her hands on the table, as if to hold it down—like if she didn't, it might just float away. "Of course, Katie's father and I are going to support her in whatever major she decides on. We just want to make sure she's considering all the factors."

What factors do you think she's overlooked? Rell wanted to ask this little woman with her precise hairdo, its complicated layers. She and Katie looked nothing alike except for that hair—they had the exact same three shades of blond worked through the exact same mousy brown, the same starburst of platinum exploding from the crown of their skulls.

Once again, Rell caught the flicker of movement out of the corner of her eye—on the floor this time, by the heating grate. So that's where the mice were getting in.

"For instance, an art degree from, say, the Rhode Island School of Design, or Pratt, definitely holds some weight in the world, in terms of establishing a career," Sandra was saying. "But that's not what Deep Canyon College is known for, is it? What your school is known for is its phenomenal environmental science program."

Was it this woman's tone? Her diction? The odd way she sat there, perched on that ugly chair with its plastic upholstery, awaiting Rell's response? Whatever it was, it was clear here Katie's mother considered Deep Canyon College a joke. This school that Rell had sacrificed so much to attend, and to which she would likely be in debt, in more ways than one, for the rest of her life.

"You know," Rell said, "what Deep Canyon is really well known for is its adventure education program."

Katie's mom laughed, like this was hilarious, that such a thing even existed. Imagine! That the people responsible for your life when you hiked the Grand Canyon or shot the rapids on the Platte or wound up inconveniently buried beneath an avalanche in the course of your ski vacation in Vail even *went* to school. Imagine that they even had lives!

That's when their resident rodent chose to mouse its way up and out of the stove's gas burner and behind the spice rack. Quickly, Rell stepped away from the table and leaned back on the kitchen counter, blocking Sandra's view.

"Honey," she said, speaking to Katie now, "when you look back, don't you want to know that you made the right decision?"

Katie turned to Rell. She was trying to communicate something, but what? An apology, maybe, for the way she'd used her mother's phrase that morning?

No. Katie had wanted something from Rell then, and she wanted something from her now: she wanted someone to see her the way she saw herself, to keep the influence of her mother's presence, its sheer force, from distorting her own self-concept.

Rell thought of her own mother, the way she'd tried to talk her out of going West—the way she'd tried to convince Rell that if she moved away from home, if she sacrificed in-state tuition, if she chose some fancy liberal arts school over home-cooked dinners and free laundry, she'd regret it for the rest of her life.

As much as Rell wanted to leave Katie, her mom, and the mouse to their own devices, she couldn't help but send Katie a pulse of sympathy, of approval, even as the echo of her words from earlier that day still hung in the air. *When you look back on this,* Rell thought, *trust me, you'll give yourself a round of fucking applause.*

Sandra had turned to Rell now too. "In any case," she said, "I just want you to know how happy I am that there's a responsible older woman around."

Rell smiled at that (Why? Why couldn't she not smile at someone who was smiling at her?) but inside, the needle of some internal indicator ticked over the line. Like, what was Katie, some sort of toddler? Rell watched as Sandra reached into her purse, pulled out a card, and then slid it across the table. "If anything comes up," she said, "I hope you won't hesitate to give me a call."

Rell looked at Katie. Subtly, Katie shook her head.

"You know," Rell said, "I'm actually graduating next month."

"Even so," Katie's mother told her, "it's so good to know you're around."

In case what? Rell wanted to ask. Did Sandra really think she was going to be tossing off emails to her, providing status updates? Sharing recipes? Did she think they were now best buds, her and her daughter's dorm mom? It was like this whole conversation, this whole scene, had been staged as a way for Katie's mom to manipulate her, to continue to exert whatever toxic influence on Katie she had recently managed to escape.

Somewhere outside, a bass beat tracked north—*ranchera*, a staple of the barrio. The Hispanic guys always looked so serious and macho when they rocked that music, though it reminded Rell of nothing so much as polka, the silly sort of oom-pah-pah you flailed around to with someone's drunk cousin at a wedding. But when Katie's mom heard that bass, Rell could have sworn she stiffened. As if it were the mating call of some exotic predator that patrolled these dangerous climes.

Katie caught Rell's eye. This time Rell was the one to shake her head, careful to keep the movement slight. And in the course of that brief exchange, any remaining animosity between them was gone.

"Well!" Sandra stood up abruptly. "I could do with a bite."

"We should get out of here," Katie was quick to say. "Rell needs the kitchen table. It's the only place in the house there's enough room for her to work."

Her mother's ash-brown eyebrows shot up at that. "Oh? What are you working on, Rell?"

"My senior thesis."

Rell spoke the words in a flat, purely functional tone, but Katie's mom just stood there smiling that too-bright smile, as if under the glare of some very bright lights. "How interesting! Tell me, what's your senior thesis all about?"

"You know what? It's about fire. It's about how fire makes things grow. If their seeds are tough enough to take it."

Once again, Katie caught her eye. *Hang in there*, Rell thought.

Instead of pulling out her laptop when they left, Rell walked into the living room and stood to one side of the window. She watched as Katie and her mother climbed into that shiny black rental—watched the way Sandra's precise blond bob swung around as she turned to back out of the driveway and then swung back when she'd completed the maneuver, the way it lay just so. In the passenger seat beside her, Katie sat with her neck all the way back against the headrest, as if bracing herself for a collision.

Three

Dry Heat

Michelle

A WEEK AFTER THE PROTEST at the courthouse, Michelle answered the knock at the back door of the Black Cat, against her judgment, before she'd had her coffee. No one she wanted to see would have arrived so early. No one she wanted to see would even have knocked.

Standing there at the bottom of those loose-nailed steps, between the compost bin and the freebox, were two sunglassed stiffs in suits.

"Good morning, Ms. McLelland," said Suit #1.

"Nice of you to knock this time."

Suit #2 nodded, apparently in agreement. "We're here to—"

"Come in," she said. "You must be sweating your balls off out here."

Whether they were sweating their balls off or not, it was clear that their faces would never betray it, nor would they deign to crack a smile. It was a stupid thing to have said anyway—it was a dry heat, after all.

Michelle let them settle in at what passed for a kitchen table at the Cat and wiped clean the coffee grinder. She caught a glimpse of Suit #1, the near-blond, lanky one—his name, she remembered, was Bates—surreptitiously swiping the surface of the table, as if casing for it for crumbs. The other one, darker in complexion and shorter in stature—Solaz—was mildly surveying the contents of the room, that commingled chaos of kitchen implements, cubbies, papers and pamphlets, outdated computer equipment, found art, folk art, and leftist propaganda that functioned as the Cat's kitchen, dining room, and office.

The last time she'd seen these guys, six months previous, had been in a room containing nothing but three chairs and two very bright lights in the basement of a government building somewhere north of Phoenix and east of who-the-fuck-knows-where. That's where these guys had taken her in a darkened van after they'd busted into the Cat like the building was on fire and screamed at everyone to get down, two days after Dyson disappeared. She'd spent a full twenty-four hours telling them the truth, which was that she had no idea where Dyson had gone, never mind what he had done back in the day or who he had done it with. The truth had not mattered, as far as these goons were concerned; Special Agents Bates and Solaz had proven as impervious to her tears, protestations, and various epithets that day as the volcanic rocks surrounding that top-secret shithole.

Now it was as if the gestapo was making house calls, or had perhaps dropped in to borrow a cup of sugar.

Michelle filled the coffee grinder with beans. She held her finger down on the button for longer than necessary, calming herself as it shrieked, then spoke immediately into the silence. "Any progress on the big case?"

Bates took off his sunglasses, and Solaz followed suit. It was a gesture no doubt meant to make them seem less scary, but when Bates looked her in the eye, that long day underground, the fundamental fear of it, came back to her.

"We have reason to believe Dyson Lathe may still be in the area," he said.

"Well, then, maybe you could have him give me a call." She turned away again, this time to pour the hot water from the kettle over the grounds in the French press. The stream wavered as she took a breath, steadying herself.

"You've seen this?"

When she turned around, Solaz had laid a newspaper on the table and flattened it with his hand.

The cover of the local daily detailed the recent fires at the Bonner Ranch, apparently started by explosives. The news was a week old, the fires well contained now, though a haze still hung in the air north of town. Michelle pretended to study the picture of the blackened, busted cow tank, the bloody corpse of the cow beside it, the plume of smoke in the distance, studying the man's hand instead. It was a wide brown hand with pale, almost lavender fingernails anchored by perfect white half moons. Solaz's suit jacket had fallen open, unbuttoned—his sole admission to the heat—and in the blur of her peripheral vision, Michelle could see the black strap of the holster against his white shirt, the bulge of the gun below his left shoulder.

"Would you like some coffee?" she asked him.

"Hey, sure. Why not?" Solaz spoke without any trace of a regional dialect, like a newscaster, and not for the first time, she wondered where he was from. Of the two suits, he was the one she hated less. With that big nose and those hang-dog eyes, he looked like the gestapo version of Cesar Chavez.

She turned to Bates. "You?"

Bates looked off into the next room, as if she had not spoken. The message was clear, in case she'd missed it the first time: he was prepared to ignore anything she said that wasn't what he wanted to hear.

"Just sugar," Solaz added.

Michelle poured steaming fair-trade Honduran into a mug emblazoned with the words *Every Bunny Needs Some Bunny*, which of course depicted any number of adorable rabbits enthusiastically embracing one another. She ignored the sugar dish on the counter and handed the man his coffee black, looking him in the eye. She hoped her message was clear as well: they were on her turf now.

"Blain Contracting reports a burglary from their warehouse shortly before the first explosion," Bates said.

Solaz blew across the surface of his ridiculous cup. "Your boyfriend—"

"Husband."

Bates almost smiled at this.

"—has a history of setting fires."

Suddenly Michelle wanted to A) throw hot coffee in Bates's face, B) bolt from the room, or C) tattoo her forearm in some pleasing, rhythmic pattern with the staple gun on the table.

"Also," Bates said, "evidence suggests he was handy with explosives."

"If anyone is handy with explosives," she said carefully, "it's Blain."

"Mr. Lathe established the Black Cat as a center for action against the pipeline," Bates said.

"Actually, we established it together."

"He was a key player in the movement opposing the pipeline."

"He was on the same side as Vern Bonner. Why would he set off dynamite on the old man's ranch?"

Bates lifted his chin. "Maybe he was attempting to frame Blain Contracting."

Michelle set her mug down on the counter beside her. "Are you kidding?"

Solaz said, "Maybe your boyfriend is trying to turn public sentiment against developers."

"Public sentiment *is* against developers."

Bates's dark eyes settled, once more, on hers, and Michelle felt her skin prickle. Looking into Bates's eyes was like looking into still water on a moonless night.

"Then why have so few expressed opposition to the pipeline?" he asked.

Michelle pursed her lips. She would not detail the thousands of signatures, the overflowing council meetings, the surveys they'd conducted showing widespread support for the cause, contrary to the poll in the paper—which everyone knew was in the pocket of George Blain. The suits were just trying to get her off guard here, to let something slip. These stiffs, who could not, would not understand that there was nothing she was holding out on, nothing she was holding back.

She took a sip of her coffee. Then turned to add more sugar. She met Solaz's eye as she measured out a heaping spoonful and stirred it into her own cup. He acknowledged this with a nod. Whatever else she could say about him, the man wasn't stupid. "Tell me," she said, "why would Dyson stick around here with assholes like you after him?"

"Maybe he didn't want to leave without you," Solaz suggested.

Michelle looked around at the hand-woven potholders, the block-print poster from the Black Mesa protest, the reassuring clutter of recycled twist ties and spilled paper clips beside the old computer, which was covered in old band stickers: Dead Kennedys, Black Fire, and Dyson's peeling old Steal Your Face with the anarchy symbol lodged inside its skeleton's head. She looked out the kitchen window at the leaves of the elm outside, to the cottonwoods along Quartz Creek beyond. Part of her wanted to believe it—that Dyson might be somewhere close to these things that reminded her of him, that he might be near to her, biding his time. Walking through the willows that grew thick around the springs that fed the Greene, along those deer trails only he could ever seem to find. Spending his nights in that old cliff dwelling flush with the red rocks of Sycamore Canyon. But as much as she wanted to believe, she knew it wasn't true. "Remember," she said, quietly now, "when we talked before, you told me not to lie. I'm going to have to ask the same of you."

Bates shifted in his seat, almost imperceptibly. As if this small movement was all that was necessary to unkink the clockwork of his gears. "You believe George Blain is responsible for the fires at the Bonner Ranch."

"Bonner is the one who put the pipeline on hold."

"Blain owns one of the largest contracting companies in the state. He would have a great deal to lose with such a reckless gesture." Once again, Bates fixed her with those fathomless eyes. "Personally, I find that idea too extreme to be believed."

Michelle cast a glance at Solaz, who was perusing the random pamphlets someone had piled up next to the computer, the one she and Dyson had gotten donated after the immigration reform protest when a couple of local rednecks broke in and smashed up the last one. Everything at the Black Cat was like that, including the pamphlets: Something someone had donated, or maybe just left here, a mash-up of dissenting viewpoints and visions, a collective effort on the part of independent people. Yet Solaz was eyeing this clutter as if it could reveal to him the root of some mystery—proof positive, probable cause.

Bates stood. "Mind if I take a look around?"

"Actually, I do."

Here, at last, he cracked a smile, as if this was a joke on her part.

"By all means," she said, as he swept past her, "go check on those bugs you planted. We've had some pretty subversive meetings lately. Maybe you checked the schedule? The Stitch and Bitch was a real hit—not to mention the Gender-Neutral Playdate! And hey, you never know what kind of wild things you're going to hear at the Citizens for Peace Potluck."

She might as well have been speaking Chinese. She might as well have said, Why don't you take a flying fuck at a rolling donut? Why don't you take a flying fuck at the moon?

As Bates commenced to whatever pressing business he had in the library, Solaz sipped from his bunny mug, his head tilted slightly. Finally he said, "You believe George Blain does not fear the law."

"Why would he? His brother-in-law is the sheriff."

Solaz seemed to consider that. Then he picked up the pamphlet he'd been studying, from the desk beside his chair. "'Knowledge is power,'" he read. "'Stop the worldwide reptile conspiracy—resist the IMF.'"

"Hey, man," she said, "just because you're paranoid doesn't mean they're not watching you."

Solaz replaced the pamphlet on the stack of papers beside the desk. He smiled mildly, looking off. "Ms. McLelland, let me ask you something."

"Go ahead."

"Do you know the name Judi Bari?"

Michelle stared at the side of his face, transfixed. Of course she knew that name. And of course he knew that she knew it. Judi Bari was an environmental activist of Dyson's vintage. She'd helped to lead the charge to stop the clear-cutting of California's old-growth. In 1990, on a tour aimed at recruiting students for Redwood Summer, a pipe bomb had exploded under the seat of her car.

"Do you remember the accident she was involved in?"

And now Michelle was no longer at the Cat, amid the comforting chaos of thrift-store dishes and flyers and folders and old punk posters. She was a hundred feet beneath the surface of the earth in an unnamed government facility she'd been driven to in a darkened van. She was sitting across from this man with the lights in her face, screaming, crying, rocking in her chair.

"There are people," Solaz said quietly, "who say she was planning to bomb the offices of Pacific Lumber Company."

"There are people," Michelle said, just as quietly, "who believe the FBI planted a bomb in her car."

"And there are people," Solaz said, finishing the last of his coffee, "who find that idea too extreme to be believed."

Michelle looked down at the floor. It didn't matter, she realized, that Solaz was Hispanic. It didn't matter where he was from. It didn't matter that he resembled a great union leader, a man of the people. This man was an agent of the state, and what he had just given her was a warning.

When she looked up, Solaz was peering into his cup. He asked, "Is that a mouse?"

"It's supposed to be a rabbit."

Solaz smiled, the edges of his basset-hound eyes crinkling. "My daughter would like this."

Michelle wondered, was Bates listening to all this in the next room? Were others listening in elsewhere via his surveillance devices? If so, did they understand what Solaz was threatening her with here—how fascist it was, how utterly fucking illegal? Did it even matter if they did?

"Please understand," Solaz said, "the evidence against your boyfriend—"

"Husband."

"—is real, but it is not conclusive. If someone else from my bureau catches him, however, they may not bother with certain..." Solaz appeared to search for a word here. "Technicalities. If you deliver him to me, I promise I'll get him the help he needs."

Michelle set down her coffee cup carefully on the counter. Though what she wanted to do was to hurl it across the room and watch it break into shards. Ceramic shards had such well-defined edges, perfect for creating clear delineations, clean lines—so unlike what was happening here, which was all threats and innuendos, angles and implications.

Still, she wondered if those implications were true. If she helped Solaz find Dyson, would Solaz help him? Would Solaz keep the FBI from pinning this other, more conclusive crime on him? Would Solaz get Dyson the right lawyer, even, the right judge?

It was only when Michelle met his eye that she realized her error.

"You think Dyson is crazy."

Solaz said nothing. He just looked at her with those sad, nowhere eyes. Those eyes with no one inside.

She laughed at that, feeling perhaps less than 100 percent stable herself. These guys showing up on her doorstep with their ridiculous insinuations. The veiled threats from this guy, followed by the heartwarming admission that he had a daughter, that she loved bunnies. Then the sucker punch: *I can help*.

Solaz considered the palm of his hand. Her laughter, she could see, made him uncomfortable. Good. Let the silence stretch between them. Let him feel the degree to which he'd miscalculated, how far from his point of view she really stood.

Finally, he said, "You are aware of the charges."

"I am aware of the charges."

"Does a sane man blow up a dam? Or set fire to another man's property?"

Does a sane man serve a corrupt state? she wanted to ask him. Does a sane man destroy lives for a living?

"I can at least get Dyson his day in court."

Now it was Michelle's turn to smile. "Special Agent Solaz, I don't think you understand my husband."

"What don't I understand about him?"

Michelle shook her head. Everything, she wanted to say, of any consequence whatsoever. "Whatever happens," she said, "Dyson Lathe will never see the inside of a courtroom."

They were looking at each other in a way that, to an outside observer, might have suggested anything: the desire to help one another or the desire to block one another at every turn; an underlying vulnerability or the total absence of vulnerability; intimacy or confrontation. If the video stopped there—if the recording were abruptly cut—Michelle wondered, would anyone guess what happened next? If something unbelievable happened to her, right here, right now?

Solaz lifted one sturdy brown hand and slid it inside his suit jacket. Michelle's heart thumped once, hard. Solaz let his hand linger there a moment, as if hesitating.

Then he withdrew a small brown envelope. It settled on the table between them as lightly as ash.

"Ms. McClelland," he said, "you may not understand him as well as you think."

Four

Entrapment

Jenna

SURE, THEY'D HAD A THING for a minute there, but now it was over, what with Crockett dating Katie and even calling her his girlfriend, which he'd never done with anyone else, as far as Jenna knew. It's not like she even cared, because she was technically still with Scott, though she'd been trying to find a way out of that mess ever since he had insisted (or at least suggested) he move out West with her. She'd watched from a distance that spring as Katie and Crockett sat cross-legged on campus, having deep conversations; she listened to them, up late in Katie's room—even from downstairs, she could hear the bedsprings squeaking. (Rell, she noticed, had taken to sleeping with earplugs.)

Truth to tell, Jenna didn't get it; it wasn't like Katie was even all that pretty. Which was an awfully bitchy thing to say, and that's why Jenna would never say it, but she couldn't help but think it, just like she couldn't help but think that it should have been her, having those long talks with Crockett. It should have been her working up to a teakettle whistle, rocking the bed frame against the drywall in a way that was virtually guaranteed to blow their deposit.

Still, everything was fine, basically.

Right up until it wasn't.

Jenna found herself in the back of the bike shop with Crockett one day around the middle of May—not alone, exactly, but close. The weather was too hot by then to shut the door, and outside, the Deep Canyon Environmental Action Group was discussing the next steps in the fight to save the Greene. Which, despite the group's stated commitment to gender parity and inclusive communication, sounded a lot like a handful of dudes trying to talk over each other.

It was a month before the hearing on the water rights claim. The grassfires on the Bonner Ranch had been put out, but now a new fire was burning to the east, in the White Mountains, and the air was full of the taste of smoke. Somewhere out there, Dyson Lathe, Deep Canyon's most infamous alum, was still on the run. Everyone knew he'd left in the middle of the night without his truck, but that was pretty much it. How had he known the feds were coming for him? Where had he gone? Had he really been part of the crew that blew the Snoquomish Dam back in 1993?

And if so, how badass was that?

Though he'd been a central figure in the fight to save the Greene River, the man had operated largely behind the scenes. Now, almost overnight, Dyson Lathe, outlaw activist, had become a kind of folk hero, inspiring all sorts of would-be revolutionaries, those handicapped by testosterone especially. Crockett was the case in point.

He leaned on the workbench beside her, nursing a bottle of ginger beer. "Those Blain boys set fire to the old man's land."

"Maybe, right?" As far as Jenna knew, the authorities were still investigating the incident. Though who even knew what that meant.

"They killed his livestock."

"I know! So gross. That poor cow."

"Poor cow? Poor rancher. That's five grand worth of beef on the hoof." Crockett took a swig of his soda. "It ain't right."

Jenna was trying to stay focused on tightening down the brakes of the Trek that was due at two, but Crockett was not wearing a shirt, and she could not help but watch, out of the corner of her eye, the way his pecs flexed as he swallowed. Crockett's lion tattoo stared sternly at her, clutching its flag, as if chastising her for her impure thoughts.

"You kill a man's cattle, you'd better be ready to face the consequences."

"What consequences?" Jenna tried to be a good sport where boys were concerned, but the drywall upstairs at 737 Sycamore had taken a particular pounding last night, and she wasn't in the mood.

Crockett looked off, propped up on an elbow—like Clint Eastwood, maybe, before Clint Eastwood had started to look like Skeletor. An effect undercut by the halo of fuzz that had lately afflicted his head; the boy was, inadvisably, trying to grow dreads. "If that was my dad's cattle, you'd have a war on your hands."

"I thought your dad was a farmer."

"He was."

"A farmer and a rancher?"

Crockett shifted a bit. "He got screwed over in the nineties by NAFTA and went into cattle. Grassfed."

Jenna said nothing. Personally, she'd begun to suspect Crockett was lying about having grown up on a farm. Though he used countryisms like *crick* and *critter*, they always sounded put on. Back in Asheville, she had gone to school with the sort of boys who showed up to first period with manure on their boots. She'd also gone to school with the sort of boys who listened to country music and drove jacked-up trucks and claimed to hunt, but when it came down to it, had spent most of their lives in some well-heeled suburb of Charlotte.

Crockett was staring off through the open door. Outside, one of the student group's more frequent speakers was quoting Che Guevara, "the revolution is not an apple." Crockett pursed his lips and nodded, like the dude had a real point there—political movements were not, in fact, all that much akin to produce. Voices rose and fell, talking about the society of the spectacle, the need for caution in the current climate, and Jenna had to wonder: Was Crockett putting her on?

"You can only push people so far," he said.

"Before what?"

"Before they push back."

"Okay, but, like, what are you going to do? What are those people out there going to do?" Really, what was anyone going to do that hadn't already been done? She was searching around for the #10 pliers, though she could have sworn she'd just seen them. Like a few other items from the bike shop in recent weeks, they seemed to have disappeared.

"Wouldn't you like to know."

"What do you even mean by that?"

"That's for me to know and you to find out."

Jenna rolled her eyes. It was all so junior high. And yet, despite herself, she was curious: what fool move did this boy have planned? "Crockett," she said, "just tell me."

He cast a glance down the front of her shirt—a pearl snap she'd picked up for a buck at the thrift—not even bothering to hide it. "I'll tell you what."

A little spark sizzled against her skin at that. She reached for the #11 pliers in an attempt to brush it away.

"Maybe you and I should drive out Wind Valley Road tonight."

"I'm not sure your girlfriend would like that."

"My girlfriend doesn't have to know."

The hubbub of conversation outside built, died off, and rose again. Just four feet away, Jenna reminded herself, people were gathered on the reclaimed concrete benches of the campus commons, amidst the drought-resistant native yucca and agave, trying to decide whether or not they had consensus on their agenda item. She and Crockett might have been alone in here, but it wasn't like anything was going to happen between them.

And yet, part of her wanted it to. Just like part of her wanted to know how Crockett thought he was going to push back against George Blain.

"You and me could ride the pipeline route tonight. Move some boulders around."

"Crockett," she said, finally, setting the pliers aside.

For as long as she'd known him, Crockett had been obsessed with sabotaging the Wind Valley Pipeline. He talked a good game, but when it came down to it, that's all it was for him, a game. Like the boys outside and their talk of revolution; when it came down to it, all they were arguing over was the wording of a press release.

But this sort of thing wasn't a game anymore. These days, you never knew who might be listening. Who, in fact, might be a member of that very same activist group, gathered out there on the commons.

Crockett leaned toward her. "Do you have any idea how hot you'd look, running the plow on my pickup?"

Jenna could feel his breath on her neck.

"In that little checkered shirt? In those friggin' Daisy Dukes?"

She laughed a little. Though what she wanted to do was scream. "Crockett," she said.

"I'm sorry. Does it make you uncomfortable when I talk about how hot you are?"

"No!" It didn't come out the way Jenna had intended it. "It's just, you shouldn't talk about stuff like that."

"Stuff like what?"

She walked to the back door of the bike shop and shut it, blocking out the crescendo of dissent. "Illegal stuff," she said, speaking quietly now. "Like messing up excavators and vandalizing the offices of that contracting company. Seriously,

Crockett—you can't joke about stuff like that on campus anymore."

Crockett finished off his soda in one long swig. "Jenna," he said. As if it were not only her name but a problem that had plagued him, day in and day out, for months. He set the bottle down on the workbench, his gaze trained on her lips. "What are you so afraid of?"

All she could do was lift an eyebrow. In a way that, granted, might have appeared just the slightest bit sexy.

He took a step toward her and said, "'We must guard against the unwarranted acquisition of influence by the military-industrial complex.'"

"Dwight D. Eisenhower," she murmured.

Another step: "'The gross heathenism of civilization has generally destroyed nature, and poetry, and all that is spiritual.'"

"John Muir."

Crockett was standing close enough now that even in the heat of the bike shop, which was well over ninety degrees, she could feel the warmth of his body.

In a voice so soft it was almost a whisper, he said, "Those who give up essential safety to obtain a little liberty deserve neither."

"That doesn't even make sense," she whispered back.

Then he was hoisting her up onto the workbench and she was kissing him ravenously, or ravishingly, or whatever they called it in trashy romance novels when two people who had, for what felt like several lifetimes, been imagining themselves naked with each other while they were naked with other people finally fell upon one another with their mouths, like animals.

Crockett took hold of her shirttails, and in one smoldering moment, those pearl snaps snapped open like poppers on the sidewalk.

* * *

Later, trying to power through the final section for agroecology, Jenna found herself staring out of the big windows on the top floor of the library at the haze to the east that had lately overtaken the sky. She should have been thinking about microbes and nematodes, bacteria and fungi, the way those funky little mycorrhizae just knocked themselves out to clear room in the soil for roots. She should have been thinking about Scott and Katie, after what she and Crockett had just done—shamelessly, right there on the workbench, between the Allen wrenches, the WD-40, and the tangled mess of the air hose.

Scott was, after all, her high school sweetheart, the guy she'd lost her virginity to—at least that's what she'd told him, and that's what he believed. And Katie, good gravy, the girl was so in love, finally, after spending all that time hung up on Huckleberry. (Not that you'd know it, considering how many guys she'd hooked up with that winter.) Jenna should have been searching her heart for the root of her sin, or at least feeling sort of bad about it.

Instead, she was thinking about the Wind Valley Pipeline. Why was Crockett so obsessed with it? And why was he always trying to get people to sabotage it with him?

Until then, she'd figured maybe he just hadn't processed it yet, the fact that the feds were prosecuting that sort of thing—which they called "politically motivated crimes of property" and everyone else called monkey wrenching—as if it was murder, or worse than murder. But sitting there on the top floor of the library in a pool of red sunshine, she had to wonder. That tough-guy stance; those lines he'd delivered, about the old man and his cattle; the way he'd actually seemed a bit misty, listening to that poseur going on about Che. Maybe she could admit it, now that she'd gone ahead and made it with him, now that every part of her body was humming that little electric song: there were times when it seemed like Crockett was playing a part.

Mired in that smoky red sun, it occurred to Jenna, and maybe not for the first time: what if he actually was?

It was no secret the FBI was on campus that semester. Dean Shelby had gone so far as to announce it publicly that spring—that while she could not legally block certain individuals from enrolling (or officially comment on the priorities of the Department of Homeland Security regarding so-called domestic terrorism in the wake of 9/11), she felt it was her duty to inform students, faculty, and staff, as well as the community of Crest Top as a whole, that there were government agents deep under cover at Deep Canyon College.

Jenna rose and walked to the back issues of the school's periodicals. Working her way down the alphabet, she found the cut-away box labeled *Earth Uprising*. The newer issues didn't advocate tree-spiking or chaining yourself to timber gates the way these old ones did, but that sort of direct action was part of the history of the organization, and the organization was part of the history of Deep Canyon, and so these back issues remained here on the top floor of the library, far from the ground-floor tours for prospective freshmen and their parents, for those who knew where to find them.

The old images were fuzzy, the layout a bit wonky. The earliest issues of the journal, Jenna knew, had been laid out in this very library back in the day, before it had low-E windows and geothermal heating and cooling and solar-powered everything. The original issues were hardly more than zines. Not unlike this random stack of publications sitting beside them—unlabeled, unboxed, and uncategorized—entitled *Caterwaul*.

Which, upon closer inspection, appeared to offer some helpful pointers on setting fires.

Jenna looked up, suddenly paranoid that someone had seen her standing there. Crockett, maybe—because what if he really was FBI? What if he started talking to her again about monkey wrenching excavators and blocking the Wind Valley Pipeline? What if he leaned in and lifted her up onto the bookshelf, sending all those old radical periodicals sliding off onto the floor?

What if he started talking revolution to her, the way he did, as if it was something sexy?

She'd do it, whatever he wanted. That, more than anything, was what scared her.

* * *

And the more Jenna thought about it, the more convinced she became. Because there were things about Crockett that had never really added up. The way he claimed to be attending college on a scholarship and paying his rent with work-study but was always throwing money around at the bar. Sure, he made some cash selling goat milk at the school farm stand, or so he claimed—Jenna had never seen milk of any sort on those tables—but did that really explain it? And what about the way he'd antagonized the old cowboy at the German Jen that night? It was like he was actively trying to make Deep Canyon college students look bad.

And where the hell were the bike tools that kept disappearing during their shift?

"Paging Jenna."

Jenna looked up. She was having dinner with Scott.

"Paging Jenna Washburn, please pick up the white paging phone."

Oh, that Scott. Such a cut-up! Employing a nearly extinct meme like that. Next thing you knew, he'd be telling her about some really hot new cassette tape, some clever computer hack that involved programming in DOS. She smiled, feeling her teeth clench. Scott had made spaghetti again, and even stuck a pink carnation in a Coke can on the table between them.

"How's the sauce?" he asked.

"The sauce is great." The sauce was terrible. Scott was a terrible cook. But he did all the cooking and the cleaning and the shopping too, so she didn't have to, because she was in school. Even though he was in school now too.

"How was work?"

It was awesome, she wanted to say. I made it with Crockett in the back of the bike shop. By the end, I was all tangled up in the air hose. Just thinking about it makes my lady parts throb. Instead, she said, "Work was fine."

"You all set with soil microbes?"

No, she thought. I spent the afternoon staring out the window, thinking in acronyms. About the FBI and the AIM, back in the sixties, about COINTELPRO and the SDS. I think Crockett's trying to entrap me. I'm not even sure I care if he is. "Yep," she said, "all set."

"That's my girl."

Jenna hated it when he called her his girl. She hated the sweetly smug way he said it. The spaghetti sauce from a jar, the bland mushrooms, the overcooked linguine, the stupid Coke can, the sickly pink flower—she hated all of this.

"What'd you do at the bike shop?" he asked. "Fix some flats?"

Jenna set down her fork.

"What?" Scott asked. "You're not saying anything."

"Why do I always have to say something? Why can't I just sit here?"

"I haven't seen you all day."

"So?" She stood, bumping the table and knocking over the soda can with the carnation. There was hardly any water inside.

"So, that's what people do." Scott's face was flushed. "They talk to each other."

"Well, maybe I don't want to do what people do."

Say it, say it, say it, came that voice in her head. *Tell him you want to break up*. Instead, she said, "You're always asking me questions. It makes me feel like you don't trust me."

"I totally trust you!" Scott was standing now too.

Well, you shouldn't, she thought.

A moment of silence passed between them. Generic apartment silence. Stupid-high-school-knickknacks-on-the-bookshelves silence. The portrait of the two of them from prom, staring in silence from the wall, like it was their wedding picture.

"You got a parking ticket," Scott told her.

And just like that, the wall she'd been building up, brick by brick, collapsed. She'd left Scott's car downtown. All day. In two-hour parking.

"Oh my god, Scott. I…"

Scott said nothing, the way he always did when he really wanted to make her feel like crap.

"I drove downtown to pay the bills," she said, trying to dig herself out but probably just digging herself in. "I walked to the bagel shop and had breakfast, and Rell was just getting off, and I was running late for my shift, so she gave me a ride back. I totally forgot I—"

Scott held up a hand. "It's all right," he said. "I already paid it."

Other guys would have been angry, or maybe condescending. Like she didn't have her shit together. Which she totally didn't sometimes, even though she always got good grades. Which Scott completely understood and never seemed to judge her for. Which never gave her any reason to actually get her shit together.

That was the thing about Scott: He loved her for the idiot she was. And maybe there was a way to break up with a guy like that, but only, Jenna had begun to suspect, if you weren't a girl like her.

She took a step toward him. Into the great, wide, windy expanse, like the Great Plains, that seemed to have opened up between them since they'd moved across the country. "Babe," she said, "I'm sorry."

He nodded a little, his face perfectly neutral. Which meant he was fighting back tears.

"It's just—" Jenna cast about for some sort of line, one she hadn't used already. But it was as if her brain had been hijacked by her body, and all her body cared about was the things it had done with Crockett's body. Things she and Crockett had agreed would never be spoken of—things that would never, ever happen again.

"I understand," Scott said. He wrapped her up in his arms the way he always did—so kindly, so carefully—and rested his chin on her head. "It's all right," he said. "Everything's going to be all right."

No, she wanted to tell him. It's not going to be all right. Everything's going to get much, much worse.

* * *

She at least succeeded in telling him, firmly, that she was going to spend the night at home because she needed to study. Which was totally true, but it was also her way of insisting on some small space of her own, the way she'd insisted on having her own room in her own house when they made the move to Arizona. But then Scott looked at her with those sad, sappy eyes and said he'd hardly seen her the last couple days, which was probably true, and so what could she do but let him kiss her.

He told her she tasted like toothpaste. And laughed, like that was funny. Like she'd brushed her teeth and rinsed with mouthwash and showered too, in the middle of the day, just because it was such a hilarious thing to do.

At which point it became clear that he wanted to make love to her, so she let him. It seemed the least she could do, after snapping at him like that and leaving his car downtown and for hating his cooking and hating their life together and also having sex with Crockett in the back of the bike shop.

But the least she could do, as it turned out, was not a whole lot. While Scott huffed and puffed and rocked through his cycle—like a washing machine, Jenna had always thought—she lay almost perfectly still. She imagined that Scott was actually Crockett and she actually couldn't move, because Crockett had tied her up. Crockett had just blown up the offices of Blain Contracting, leaving a smoldering mess in his wake, effectively destroying the Wind Valley Pipeline. He was an outlaw hero on the run, and now he'd taken her hostage and tied her to a chair in an abandoned warehouse somewhere. But Crockett couldn't help it, he was just so hot for her…

Or maybe she'd chained herself to a mining truck as part of a direct-action protest. Everyone else had given up and gone home when the police arrived with tear gas, but not her—she was too passionately devoted to saving Zeb Mountain, where she'd spent summers with her granddad learning how to shoot squirrels (this part was true). And Crockett was a federal marshal, the best of the best, and he'd been sent in to intimidate her, to convince her to leave, but instead he'd fallen in love with her and the strength of her convictions. And it was kind of wrong, what he was doing to her, all chained up like that still, but she wanted it too, she couldn't deny it any longer, and…

Then Scott was making that sort of choked weasel sound and rolling off of her.

A dry breeze swept in through the windows with the smell of immolated sap, lifting the curtains. They lay there together atop the sheets for a moment under the wind's caress. Which seemed far more sensual than anything that had just occurred between them.

Or maybe anything that had ever occurred between them.

A dog barked in a yard nearby, and someone called it inside. Out of the night, with its scent of wild things in need of chasing. Away from those coyotes in the far, high hills, laughing at the moon.

"You still there?" Scott asked, at last.

And the way he said it, the way his voice broke, almost broke her.

"Yeah, babe," she said, taking his hand. "I'm still here."

* * *

She waited until Scott had fallen asleep to collect her clothes from off the floor, to dress in the dark and slip out of the room without shutting the door, lest she wake him. Jenna didn't want to say good-bye. Jenna just wanted to be gone.

She walked the half mile or so home around ten, down the familiar streets of the barrio, past its small houses and tall elms, apartment buildings and trailer parks, with a red moon hanging low in the sky. Just an effect of the smoke that had darkened the skies over Crest Top these last few days, but still, it felt like the all-seeing eye of some all-seeing god who knew her every shitty thought.

She was a terrible person for cheating on Scott. For letting him love her without loving him back. For taking his hand and telling him she was there instead of telling him the truth, which was that she was miles, years, light-years away from him. Jenna knew she was a terrible person, but the thing was, she didn't feel like a terrible person. She felt like the same person she'd always been, the one her parents had always been so proud of. The girl whose SAT scores were good enough to crack the *Princeton Review*'s top twenty, but who'd come out West to this little hippie school instead; who knew how to fix most things on bikes and cars but occasionally forgot where she'd parked her boyfriend's Corolla; who loved flailing around in the crowd at rock concerts but also sitting home alone on the back-porch steps playing old-time mountain music like someone's toothless Appalachian granny.

The problem, Jenna felt, was not with her. The problem was with all these boys who always wanted her attention.

And maybe this was why she'd stayed with Scott so long—so she wouldn't have to say no. First high school boys and then college boys, coffee shop boys and bar boys. What came next? Office boys? Science boys? Stuck-way-the-hell-out-on-this-organic-farm boys? Was there ever going to be a point in her life when all these boys just sort of went away? Or would she have no peace until her face got craggy, her ass went flat, and her boobs sagged toward her belly button like a couple of tube socks loaded down with rocks?

What she needed, she decided, was a ranch in the Bradshaw Mountains—a place so far from a city of any size that she'd never have to say no to a boy again, never have to feel herself falling toward his need. She'd keep horses and chickens and ruminants, with only one male of each species, a stud. And maybe she'd have a cowboy, lean and long like Crockett, with a ranch of his own, but way the hell out somewhere, like Montana. And he'd want to come live with her and raise babies, but he wouldn't be able to leave that ranch of his, and she wouldn't be able to leave hers, though she loved him, and maybe actually he'd be the one with the stud. And once a year in the spring, he'd drive that beautiful animal across the country to service her mares, and while he was there, he'd service her too. And then—this was the important part—he'd pack up and kiss her good-bye and leave her all alone to pick the banjo after supper, singing those sad old lonesome love songs that had somehow always made her feel happy.

All in all, though, it seemed unlikely. She'd probably wind up marrying Scott, or some guy just like him. Some guy who was just so nice that when he got down on one knee in the worst possible way, in the most embarrassing possible place, she wouldn't be able to say no.

Unless Scott found out that she'd slept with Crockett. Really, that seemed the easiest way out. But what if Scott was so nice that he didn't break up with her, even then? That would be, seriously, the worst-case scenario. And then Katie would hate her and call her a slut, and everyone else would too, especially when they found out Crockett was FBI, if he was.

And then Jenna was pushing in through the back door to 737 Sycamore Street, into the light of the kitchen, where Katie was studying what appeared to be a class handout. Katie looked up at her, and in the slow-motion moment before Jenna could get a smile on her face, she felt like a fish hit with a dynamite charge, floating up to the surface, stunned.

"Hey," said Katie.

"Hey!" Jenna said. "Long time no see." She couldn't actually remember the last time she'd seen Katie. Weeks, at least—since then, Katie had shaved off half her hair and lost that twee little fimo-bead necklace. "Hitting the books?"

"Sort of," Katie replied. Somewhat weirdly. While Jenna watched, she folded up her reading material and slid it into a side pocket of the messenger bag at her feet. Carefully, almost casually, she flipped the bag's top flap up and over it. But not before Jenna had glimpsed those two sets of pliers poking up from the pockets on the side.

"I thought you were spending the night at Scott's."

"Nope! I've got my soil science final tomorrow."

Katie didn't act like she'd even heard that; apparently, it took all her powers of concentration to keep that sour look on her face.

Jenna hung her own bag on the hook by the door, slid her books onto the table across from Katie, and then stepped up to the cupboard and dug through the boxes of tea, looking for something with caffeine. But the look on Katie's face stayed with her, like an afterimage. Her roommate wasn't happy to see her.

Did she know? Had she guessed?

Don't be a dipshit. It wasn't like she had a big red A on her forehead, and it wasn't like Crockett was going to tell his *girlfriend* about their little escapade in the back of the bike shop.

Maybe the better question was, what had Katie been doing when Jenna walked in? Also: What had she been so quick to slip into her bag? And what the heck was Katie doing with those two sets of pliers? Katie had the mechanical aptitude of a bonobo. (Which perhaps sounded uncharitable, but Jenna had actually seen her at a party once trying to open a bottle of wine with a can opener.)

Jenna recalled that conversation she'd had with Crockett: *What can anyone do that hasn't already been done?*

Wouldn't you like to know.

Jenna stood there for a moment, looking off into the darkness of the cupboard as if it were an oracle, a Magic 8 Ball, that was going to spit out an answer: Talk to Katie. Don't talk to Katie. Of course, if Jenna did talk to her, she'd say something stupid—Katie would know. If she didn't already. Crockett was probably seeping out of Jenna's pores now; shower or no shower, Scott's efforts notwithstanding, she was probably atomizing Crockett's love juice into the air like a friggin' mister.

But in another moment, Katie was going to get up from that table, and chances were, it would be weeks before Jenna saw her again.

"Hey," Jenna said as she set up a cup of Earl Grey, trying to sound casual, "how're things with Crockett?"

Katie had already slung her bag over her shoulder. But she stopped at the entrance to the hallway, leaning into it. "Good. How're things with Scott?"

"Good. Kind of hard, but you know. The good kind of hard."

Katie did her best to look sympathetic, but really she just looked smug, like she knew nothing at all about the good kind of hard. Jenna felt both relieved and ashamed. Katie had no idea.

"I just wanted to say, if you ever need anyone to talk to, I'm here."

"About what?"

"I don't know. Crockett? We do spend a lot of time together at work." Almost immediately, Jenna could see that this was the wrong thing to say. She tried again. "It seems like all he ever talks about these days is the pipeline."

"That's because he's an activist. That's what activists do. They get obsessed."

Oh, yes—Jenna had managed to forget that Katie was an activist now too. "It just seems like there's something off about him lately."

"What do you mean, off?"

The problem was, it wasn't anything Jenna could put her finger on. It wasn't like she'd really caught Crockett in any kind of lie; it just seemed, intuitively, like he was lying. And in light of the dean's announcement that spring, that seemed like something Katie should be aware of. Especially since she was getting the sort of nookie on a regular basis that turned your brain into Jell-O salad with nuts. "Honey pie," she said. "Just listen to me, all right? I don't want to see you get hurt."

Katie swung her messenger bag around behind her and tightened the strap. "Jenna," she said, "I realize you may still have feelings for Crockett."

"Oh no," Jenna said, "really, it's just—"

Katie took a step closer. "In fact, it's perfectly natural."

Jenna opened her mouth and closed it again, like a fish.

Katie took a step closer, in front of the room's single bulb, casting a long shadow along the wall. "But Jenna?" she said.

"Yeah?"

"As one feminist to another?" Katie swept her hair off her shoulder. "Stay the fuck away from him."

And with that, she turned and walked away down the hall.

Jenna stood there in the kitchen for a while, just listening to the sounds of traffic through the open windows. Just breathing in the scent of a smoldering forest—somewhere to the southeast, she had heard, toward Show Low. Fifty thousand acres, 50 percent contained.

Jenna remembered Scott, the way his voice had broken that evening, asking if she was still there. The way he'd held her close and rested his chin atop her head. Dear, sweet Scott, who'd bailed her out of every stupid thing she'd ever done, and who'd gotten no more than the ass end of her love for years now. How could she do this to him?

Jenna sat down heavily, her head in her hands. Then, finally, opened to the chapter on microbes. But who was she kidding? She was a basket case, her line of thought hopelessly lost, entangled with the air hose from the bike shop and that pink carnation from dinner and the frayed edges of that torn-out sheet of notebook paper on the table before her, devoid of anything but those strangely contorted doodles, which it seemed as if someone else must have drawn.

How could you straighten out a mess like that?

Where did you even begin?

Five

Rad Summer

Rell

IT WAS A WEEK OUT from graduation when Rell's mom called with the news.

"Dyson something. He went to your school, back in the seventies."

"Yeah, I know him. I mean, I know *of* him. What happened?" Why had Rell even bothered to pick up the phone? Her mother was the only one who ever called the landline. Her mother, who could kill a half hour talking about so-and-so's puttanesca recipe she saw on TV.

"They found him in Colorado." On the other end of the line, her mother turned down the television. "He had a gun. He turned it on himself, they're saying."

"What? When?"

"Just this weekend. It's right here on Channel Two. 'Christopher Mason, known as Dyson Lathe, from Crest Top, Arizona, a graduate of Deep Canyon College.' They say he was a terrorist." Her mother paused and lowered her voice. "Gabby, they didn't teach you anything like that, did they? Terrorism things?"

"Mom…" There was nothing attached to the word, no possible reply.

"If I'd known people like that went to that school, I never would have let you go."

"You didn't let me go, remember? I paid my own way."

Silence, then a sniffle. *Fuck me, is she crying now?* "You're such a willful little shit," her mom said. "You know that? You've always gotten what you wanted. Which is great. Don't get me wrong. All I ever wanted was to be on *The Ed Sullivan Show*, and we all know how far that got me. But I'm your mother, and I want you safe."

"Mom, it's so safe in Pittsburgh, I'm falling asleep just thinking about it."

Her mother honked into a Kleenex. "When all those student loans come due, you might appreciate a little stability. I've been talking to Dr. Sillman about this summer—"

"I'm not sure about this summer."

"You're going to keep working in the bagel shop?"

Rell allowed her eyes to drift shut. "I'm not sure about that either."

"It sounds like you're not sure about a lot of things."

"Mom, I'll see you Wednesday, okay?"

Getting off the phone with her mother was never easy. When Rell managed to at last—after she'd gone back over the directions from the hotel, the schedule for the weekend, and the fact that, yes, it was May, which meant that Crest Top was hot—she stood there in the hallway beside that clunky old cordless feeling dazed and confused, the way she often did after talking with her mom, but also vaguely alarmed. It wasn't enough that she was graduating in a few days' time and would soon have to deal with her mother in person. Now she had Channel Two News to deal with as well.

Rell was the only one home that day. Which was more or less the sitch on a daily basis since Katie had hooked up with Crockett, because Jenna, though she was never willing to admit it, basically lived with Scott. But Jenna at least dropped in here and there to throw out the wilted produce she'd accumulated in the fridge. Katie had all but disappeared.

There was no one around for Rell to share this with. No one she could even think of to call. And the fact that she'd gotten this news from her mother really just went to show how isolated, in her final semester, she'd allowed herself to become.

Maybe because the handful of friends she'd managed to claim in the split with Trevor seemed like they were on a different wavelength these days. There'd been an epidemic of engagements in the last month alone, and everyone seemed to have lined up fascinating jobs in fascinating places. The Deep Canyon College class of 2005 would scatter to the directions, like seeds to the wind, come the first of June.

The lease at 737 Sycamore was up the same day, and lately Rell had begun to toy with the idea of signing on for another six months. Because that old rattrap had grown on her, maybe. Because it seemed strange that she had yet to spend a summer in Crest Top. Because returning to Pittsburgh, postgrad, couldn't help but feel like sort of a relapse. But mainly, let's face it, because she had yet to line up anything more fascinating than this gig as a dentist's receptionist her mother was so seriously psyched for her to take.

The phone burbled beside her. Of course there was something her mom had forgotten. Of course it couldn't wait until Wednesday. Rell picked up in a fit of pique. "Mom—"

"Is Katherine Callahan available."

"I'm sorry, may I ask who's calling?"

"Special Agent Bensoncourt with the Federal Bureau of Investigation."

Rell rested her forehead against the wall, looking down at the dust bunnies that had accumulated there. "I haven't seen her today. In a while, actually." Like, months. "Is everything okay?"

"To whom am I speaking?"

"Rell Kendall. I'm Katie's roommate."

"Could you spell that, please?"

Rell did, doing her best to speak slowly, clearly, not to sound alarmed. She took down the man's number, promised to call if she saw her roommate, and once again hung up.

When was the last time she *had* seen Katie? She only ever seemed to come home late at night and was always gone by morning. The girl had a cell phone—her parents covered it—but either she never carried it or she never answered it. According to Jenna, she'd also pretty much stopped going to class.

Which explained, maybe, how Rell found herself standing in Katie's room that day.

The place was like a time capsule from early March. The receipts from the bar, the band flyers, the empty pouches of rolling tobacco—the homework and handouts from spring block—the dresses of various themed evenings in casual disarray on the floor—Katie's chaotic paintings, in various stages of completion, the tubes of paint curled up on the easel—the mandala tapestry on the wall. It looked like nothing had moved in months.

What had Rell expected to find? A note, perhaps, like the one the early settlers had left when they mysteriously vacated their colony in Virginia—*Gone to Croatan?*

On a whim, she popped open the door to Katie's closet. And blinked, confronted with a sheet of clear plastic. Rell lifted one section and was amazed to discover that the entire room had been lined with this stuff, hung with blue duct tape. Gone were the boxes of keepsakes and old stuffed animals Rell recalled. The space had been cleared of everything except a little card table, also covered in plastic. Sitting on this card table were a spool of copper wire, two pairs of pliers, a nine-volt battery, and a veritable flock of old-fashioned kitchen timers—Rell counted ten of them.

She pushed past the plastic, picked up one of the timers, turned the dial, and listened to it tick. The sound struck her as goofy, like a cartoon bomb—Acme Company biz. But then she spotted the manual, beneath this mysterious clutch, entitled *How to Set Fires Using Electrical Timers.*

Rell had a flash then of Crockett, that night at the German Jen. What he'd said about the bulldozers lined up down Goldwater Highway, waiting to lay the pipe that would kill the Greene: *It'd be shame if a few of those bad boys wound up out of commission tonight.* And then a flash of Katie, the way she'd smiled that day when they'd walked home from his house.

Katie and Crockett, Crockett and Katie—the combination struck Rell, suddenly, as akin to fuel and fire. A cigarette butt dropped from a car window, still smoking, and a dry forest, piled high with dry pine.

The front door opened. Quickly, Rell shut Katie's closet and slipped out of Katie's room, back out onto the landing, where she could hear someone banging pots and pans around in the kitchen. She made her way downstairs to find Jenna leaning into the bleak light of the fridge, looking tear-worn and tired and generally pretty much like shit.

"You all right?"

Jenna looked up, her baby blues filling with glassy sadness, as if on cue.

"What happened?"

Jenna pulled the carton of eggs from the fridge. "You know," she said. "No biggie. No big whoop. It's just kind of hard to break up with someone when they refuse to even acknowledge what's happening."

Rell backed up to the kitchen counter. "Scott's not taking it well, I take it."

Jenna cracked an egg against the lip of a pan. "I'd say he's pretty much not taking it at all."

"So you tell him that you need to talk—"

"And he walks into the bedroom and turns on the computer. Says he's doing research."

Rell hopped up onto the counter. "So you try to talk to him while he's on the computer…"

Jenna turned down the heat on her eggs. "I swear to god," she said, "it's like talking to a wall. I mean, how can you, just, act like…" Tears were dripping into the mess in the frying pan, sizzling. "We've been together since…"

Jenna was quietly losing it now, her eyes squeezed shut, and the spatula beside the burner was melting. Rell crossed the kitchen in two steps, wrapping Jenna in one arm even as she reached around to shut off the gas with the other.

They stood there in the kitchen with the burned eggs and the smell of melted plastic and the heat of the day coming on. Summer that year having arrived hot on the heels of snow. *Fucking Crest Top,* Rell thought, perhaps inappropriately. One day you were freezing your ass off and the next your house was on fire.

Jenna pulled away. "Oh jeez, did I snot on you?"

"Never mind. You haven't seen Katie, have you?"

"Kind of."

It seemed an odd response. "Jenna—question."

"Is this about the gas bill? I've got my checkbook right here."

"No, it's—"

"Or the garden? I'm staying for the summer, for sure. Did you decide?"

"Not yet, but listen—I just got a call for Katie."

Jenna blinked.

"From the FBI."

Rell's roommate looked down at the floor. As if those ugly brown-and-yellow squares with their divots full of ancient foodstuffs were suddenly the most fascinating thing in the world. Her mouth worked, quirking her dimples. "Rell," she said, "do you have a minute?"

As Jenna boiled water for yerba maté, Rell filled her in on both the phone call and the contents of Katie's closet. By the time they were blowing that grassy, pungent steam from their cups, Jenna was sharing her suspicions about Crockett. Rell held one hand to her temple as she listened, less to massage the tension that had accrued there than simply to provide some support.

"You think Crockett is lying about his dad?" she said.

"Have you ever heard of a farmer turned rancher?"

Rell shrugged. "As far as land-use patterns go, it's not implausible for Nebraska. Whereas out here, I'd say, yeah, totally, that doesn't make sense. It's all about topsoil, you know? And precipitation."

Jenna heaved a sigh, indicating the great patience she was calling upon here. "Okay, but listen. I grew up with country boys. Farm boys. Crockett isn't like that."

"Like what?"

"Like them."

"How?"

Jenna looked off. "Honestly, I don't even know what it is. Maybe he just talks too much."

Rell regarded Jenna over the rim of her cup. This was the big thing she had to share with her? Like she, Rell, did not have a metric shit ton of better things to do with her limited amount of time before that short walk, come the following weekend, across the John Muir Memorial Amphitheater stage?

Jenna leaned forward, intent now. "You've seen how he is, always running his mouth. You remember that night at the German Jen?"

"How could I forget." It wasn't a question. In the long dry spell Rell had endured that spring—following the long dry spell that, in retrospect, had ended her relationship—she'd thought back over that night with Crockett more times than she cared to admit.

"Crockett's always trying to get people to do things like that, to monkey wrench the pipeline. It's like he's obsessed."

"And now Katie thinks she's a radical."

"Exactly! That's what I'm saying—it's Crockett. He's setting her up."

"But why would he do that?"

Jenna lifted one hand, like this should have been obvious. "It's this thing with Dyson. He shot himself. When they caught up with him in Colorado."

"I heard." Rell tried not to let it sound sharp, but she could not help but be reminded that no one but her mother had bothered to inform her of this hot news item, which surely must have made its way around Deep Canyon College faster than a case of the crabs.

"Dyson made the FBI look bad. Because he got away with all that stuff, way back when. And he kind of got away this time too. They want to catch somebody so they can shut our school down. Just like they shut down the American Indian Movement and the Black Panthers."

Now Rell had both hands on her temples. "Seriously?"

"What?"

"That was back in the sixties."

"Rell, Guantanamo."

"All right, but—"

"Warantless wiretapping."

"Well, yeah, but—"

"No, seriously—since 9/11, all these crazy government agencies have gotten tons of cash. I read about it on *Slate*. They're targeting animal rights activists, environmental activists, all kinds of people—domestic terrorism, they call it. That's why the FBI's at our school. You know that, right?"

Yes, even Rell knew that, though she'd hadn't thought much about that email from the dean's office since the start of the semester. Because what was the point in thinking about it? She would only have fallen down the same rabbit hole that Jenna here had.

"Okay," Rell said, "fine. Let's say, for the sake of argument, that there is some kind of shady government conspiracy to shut down our school. Let's say that Crockett, or whatever his name is, really is an undercover agent who's trying to set someone up. Even if we go with all that—why Katie?"

Jenna chewed her lip. "Isn't her mom a senator or something?"

If anything comes up, I hope you won't hesitate to give me a call. It was a gesture so strange that Rell had actually looked up Katie's mom—Sandra Callahan represented the state of New Hampshire, somewhat ineffectively, according to various reports. She was up for reelection next year; the GOP had their sights on her seat.

And just like that, Rell was falling, like Alice into Wonderland—into a place where up was down, down was up, and all those kitchen timers in Katie's closet might just sprout wings and fly away. She had the backs of her upper arms on the table now, her fingertips resting on her face—like if she didn't keep it firmly affixed there, it might just slide off onto the table. "But if Crockett's trying to set Katie up, why have that agent call her? Wouldn't that blow Crockett's cover?"

"Maybe Katie's started to suspect him, so the other guy is trying to throw her off his scent."

"How would that help? Like, if the whole idea is entrapment, why would they be trying to scare her right now, before she's actually done whatever it is they're setting her up to do?"

"Maybe she *has* done something. Something we don't know about yet."

Rell considered Jenna's red-rimmed eyes, her half-eaten plate of eggs, the split ends she'd accumulated over the last few months. Rell decided to try a different tack. "So, if Crockett's undercover, what's up with his whole backyard farming operation? Not exactly low pro."

"He's not trying to be low pro, he's trying to be popular. As in, like, meet everyone." Jenna laughed a bit, despite herself. "I mean, who isn't going to talk to a dude who's out walking his goat?"

Rell smiled. At least she'd managed to take the edge off Jenna's funk. Poor Jenna, trying to break up with Scott, who was clearly stuck like a burr on her cute little butt. She'd probably been up late crying, staring at the ceiling, while Scott lay there beside her snoring obliviously, the way dudes did. Who knows what kind of nonsense she'd managed to convince herself of?

"I tried to talk to Katie about it," Jenna was saying, "but she's so crazy about Crockett. It's like, if you say anything about him, she just shuts down. Which is weird, because we used to talk all the time about Huckleberry."

"Who?"

Jenna lifted one shoulder, a half shrug. "This boy she sort of had a thing with back in the fall. Kind of like Crockett, but I don't know—older. And more real."

"More real how?"

Jenna laid one hand on the table between them. "Just…" And then she stopped. "Rell, I know this whole thing sounds crazy. But there's something phony about Crockett."

"Like, beyond the fact that he's sort of a hustler?"

Jenna's brow furrowed. "A hustler? How?"

Rell studied Jenna's face. Was it possible that she didn't see it? The way Crockett hit on practically every girl he met? How manipulative he was about it?

Was it possible, perhaps, that Jenna still had a thing for Crockett—even after everything she'd just said?

Possible, even, that everything she'd just said was no more than an attempt to get Katie to break up with Crockett, in some deviously roundabout way, through Rell?

Rell stood. If she fell any farther down this rabbit hole, she'd start believing that Dick Cheney orchestrated the attack on the Twin Towers, aliens had infiltrated the highest levels of government, and there were authentic spiritual experiences to be had in the course of a Sedona Pink Jeep Tour. "Let's focus here. Do you think Katie's over at Crockett's right now?"

"Maybe. But if he's undercover, we can't let him know that we know."

"I don't even know what we know."

Jenna pursed her mouth, as if to disagree, but then appeared to think better of it.

"Where was the last place you saw Katie without him?"

Jenna considered. "Probably down at the Cat."

* * *

Rell had hit up the Black Cat for a few shows over the years, but she'd never just stopped by during the day to poke around. On its handmade flyers and brochures—scattered across community boards and coffee shops around town—the place advertised itself as a center for activism and education, an egalitarian institution that clothed the homeless (via its freebox) and fed the poor (via Food Not Bombs). What Rell found was a sad little secondhand library presided over by a few sullen, punked-out teenagers from the local high school.

These kids looked up at her approach but made no move to greet her, nor did they bother to return a friendly hello. With their cunning faux-hawks and sideswept bangs, they seemed to regard her, she realized, the way she'd once regarded her older sister, with her heavy black eyeliner and black velvet vests. But for what? Her baggy jeans and Birkenstocks? Listen, she wanted to tell them, I was holding my own in mosh pits while you were still sucking on Otter Pops. Have some fucking respect.

Rell drifted between the stacks, picking up pamphlets on the adverse long-term health effects of mercury amalgam fillings, chem trails and crop dusters and neonicotinoids. The whole world, it seemed, was out to kill her—not to mention the birds and the bees and the Mexican gray wolf. On a card table in the corner, there was a display dedicated to efforts to support Native activists up on the rez, as well as one showing pictures from various protests to *Save the Greene!* She spotted a girl who could only have been Katie, near the back of a cluster of protesters in Quartz Creek Park. The photo must have been from the fall, because the yellow leaves of the cottonwood trees were strewn about their feet; Katie was leaning back slightly, the sun in her hair, wearing a striped sweater over a polo shirt, as if she stood on the deck of a listing ship. The girl in the picture was holding one hand of a grinning backpack puppet wearing a cowboy hat, which was clearly supposed to be George Blain. She looked more like she was in a school play than a protest.

Through the open doorway, Rell could see the Cat's kitchen counter was piled high with cabbage—culled, no doubt, from the infamous Safeway dumpster. Rumor had it the store's produce manager had cut a deal with the Cat on the sly to call before filling its dumpster with produce. The idea was to save the volunteers from Food Not Bombs the trouble of diving in under cover of night and inviting the curiosity of raccoons. Recently, Rell had heard, that manager's manager had gotten wind of the deal and fired him. So now the Black Cat's volunteers, in their efforts to feed the hungry, were back in the same boat as the raccoons.

Outside in the driveway, two kids were unloading still more cabbage from the bed of a little blue pickup. They were just as young as their counterparts out front, and just as punk, but Rell realized she recognized one of them.

"What up, Arin."

"What up, Rell."

Arin wore a cap-sleeved babydoll tee with the feminist power symbol silkscreened on it, somewhat incompletely, with a pair of cut-off denims and those same heavy black combat boots. The tall kid beside her wore his hair in a topknot, shaved around the sides, a bolt of some sort in his ear. "Hey," he said. "Gabriel."

"No kidding," said Rell. "That's my name. Sort of. Like, on my birth certificate."

"Rell," Gabriel said. "You need a cabbage?" And then, before she could reply: "Catch."

Rell did, but barely. Gabriel had tossed her possibly the largest cabbage in the truck, and it weighed as much as a bowling ball. But when he smiled at her it was so genuine she couldn't help but smile back.

"Never mind this asshole," Arin said. "You want a cup of tea or something? It's self-serve inside."

Arin, as it turned out, had volunteered at the Black Cat in some capacity since its inception, but she was now obligated to do so for Food Not Bombs because the late Dyson Lathe had given her his truck on that condition.

"So you knew that guy, Dyson?" Rell tried to make it sound casual. Of course, everyone would have heard the news by now.

Arin eyed her with an expression Rell couldn't quite name. "Sure. Everyone here did. Why don't we go sit out back?"

Out back, a sofa had been hauled up onto the Cat's makeshift stage, where someone had spray-painted the words *Rad Summer of the Indigo Children* across the plywood floor. Which meant what, exactly? This was, Rell realized, what drove her crazy about the place: the sense that everybody here was in on some kind of big secret.

"Seems a shame, the way it went down." Rell cast a glance at Arin. "What were they after him for? Do you know?"

Arin sipped her tea, as if choosing her words. "He was part of the crew that blew the Snoquomish Dam. But what they got him for was the fires—lumberyards and plywood plants. In the nineties, the big logging companies were selling off the last of the old-growth and these thousand-year-old trees were just rolling down the highway outside Eugene. Dyson used to tell me about it." She cocked her head. "The trees, at least. The arsons, we figured out. Nobody ever got hurt, but the feds were calling him a terrorist. Or, eco-terrorist. Which sounds cooler, right?"

Rell felt the words settle into the pit of her stomach. She looked around. "Arin, can I ask you something?"

Arin lifted one dark eyebrow. "What, you think this place is bugged?"

The thought hadn't even occurred to Rell. She licked her lips. "Is it?"

"Sure. That's why we're sitting outside."

Of course it was. The Black Cat was on the FBI watch list. Her school was on the FBI watch list. The whole damn town probably was. And Katie was assembling god-knows-what in her closet. Rell squeezed her eyes shut.

"Have you seen Katie around?"

"Rell?"

If not for her voice, Rell would have had no idea who this girl was. She'd appeared from around the side of the house holding a cabbage under each arm, wearing a wife-beater over a black bra and a knee-length pair of army fatigues. Katie—this Katie—bore no more than a passing resemblance to the girl in the photograph Rell had seen from last fall; she'd shaved her head on one side and dyed those salon-blond highlights green.

"What up, Katie."

"It's K now," she said.

"Kay? Like, Mary Kay?"

"No. Just, like, K. The letter K." Her voice seemed a bit hoarse, her eyes puffy, like maybe she had a cold.

"Okay," Rell said. "Cool. How are you doing these days?"

"Fine."

"I've missed having you around." Even as Rell uttered that platitude, she realized it was true.

"Yeah, I've just been—" Katie (Rell could not call her K) cleared her throat. "I've been busy." Her roommate's voice had thickened, and Rell could see now that Katie didn't have a cold; Katie had been crying.

And with that, everything Rell had come here to say, everything she had come to confront Katie about, seemed to evaporate—she just wanted to give this fierce-looking girl, standing there bravely with her cabbages, a hug. Arin turned to Rell, clearly wondering if she should leave them alone. But then Katie asked Arin if she and Gabriel needed help with the soup.

"Naw," Arin said. "I think we've got it." She stood up from the couch and stretched.

Rell stood too. "How's it going with Crockett these days?"

Katie stilled for a moment, as if weighing her words. Or perhaps how much longer she could stand there with those cabbages under her arms looking tough and cool before she had to shift their weight. Finally, she said, "Don't act like you don't know."

Rell studied her face. Remembering that exchange with Jenna: *I don't even know what we know.* "I know he's got some pretty dumb ideas."

Katie just laughed, short and sharp. Even her laugh didn't sound like her.

Rell cast a glance at Arin. For some reason, Rell didn't want her to leave; she had the feeling that if she did, Katie would leave too. "Jenna and I—"

"How dare you."

Rell blinked. "Katie—"

"K."

"What's up with the stuff in your closet?"

"Rell," Katie said, her voice low, "what were you doing in my closet? And what are you doing here?"

Rell lifted her hands. "So I snooped. What else was I supposed to do? You never come home anymore, you never answer the phone, and I've been worried about you, okay? Jenna's been worried too. She's got some theory about Crockett, and I have no idea if it's true, but guess what? Just this morning, some guy from the FBI called for you."

Katie said nothing, but the look she gave Rell could have burned a hole right through her and out into the dry yellow weeds between the Cat and the trees along the creek. Rell lifted a hand in Arin's direction. "What do you think?" she said. "Should we fill in our friend here? Maybe you want to explain the plans for your little science experiment."

"Maybe you want to shut your mouth."

"Maybe you want to tell me what Crockett's trying to get you to do."

"What makes you think"—Katie said the words slowly—"what's in my closet"—her tone matter-of-fact—"has anything to do"—a muscle in her jaw twitched—"with Crockett?"

Now it was Rell's turn to weigh her words. "Did you hear what happened to Dyson?"

"The fuck do you know about Dyson?"

"I know he isn't here right now because he did something stupid."

"Dyson Lathe was a hero."

"Because he blew up a dam? And set some fires? And then put a gun to his head?"

"Because he had real convictions," Katie said quietly. "But that's not something you would understand, would you, Rell?"

Rell could not help but stare. What had happened to the fluffy little freshman she'd partied with that spring? The one with a bad habit of swiping *Cosmo* from the HR office at school? "A hero? Christ, Katie, the guy was a nut job."

"Whoa," said Arin. "May I just say, slow the fuck down, both of you." To Katie, she said, "I know you're all hardcore these days, K, and I'm sure Dyson really changed your life at that one party where you met him, but I've known that dude since I was thirteen, and for the record, there are things about him you'd probably just as soon not know." Arin turned to fix Rell with her dark eyes. "He did save some peoples' lives, though. People no one else gave a shit about. He also managed to decommission one of the most ecologically destructive dams in North America. Which—I don't know about you—is more than I can say."

"Listen, I'm sorry," said Rell.

Arin looked up at the sky.

"No, I mean, really."

"For fuck's sake," said Arin.

"No," Rell said, "that was judgmental, not to mention completely uninformed. I had no right to call him crazy."

"Rell, would you stop with the politically correct ass-licking?"

"I mean, what do I know? I never even met the guy. I'm just repeating what I've heard other people say"—Rell glanced at Katie here—"the same way she is."

Slowly, carefully, Katie set down her two heads of cabbage on the stage beside the couch. As if they were the two most precious things in the world to her. It was a gesture that struck Rell, for some reason, as beautiful.

"All I'm trying to do is keep Katie—"

"K." Katie almost whispered it.

"From doing something she might regret."

Rell searched her roommate's face. For a moment, she saw the old Katie there: young and, as a consequence, just a bit dumb, but a sincere person, sincerely conflicted. "Katie," she said, "when you look back—"

Katie seemed to focus on her from across some great distance. "When I look back," she said, "I'll know I did everything I could."

That bubble around her head seemed to have opened up for a split second, but Rell, in echoing the words of Katie's mother—Katie's own words to her—had said precisely the wrong thing. Now that space around Katie's head had sealed up tight again, leaving Rell and everyone else on the outside, come hell or high water or George W. Bush himself dropping in from the skies like a paratrooper. "Katie," she said, "what do you even mean by that? Like, do you even know? Whatever you've got planned—whatever you're planning to do—it's not worth the risk. Seriously. You could wind up in prison."

But Katie wasn't listening. Katie was walking away from her, through the back door of the Cat. "Do you understand what I'm saying?" Rell called after her. And then, when Katie failed to reply: "What if this guy from the FBI calls again? What do you want me to tell him?"

Katie returned to stand in the doorway. An odd expression passed over her face, the way a thin cloud passes over the sun. It wasn't fear, exactly, but—what? Then, just as quickly, it was gone. "Don't worry about it. Just stay out of my room."

"Fine." Rell had no choice but to say it to the doorway. Katie was gone.

* * *

Fine indeed, because Rell simply did not have the bandwidth for Katie's bullshit. Her mother and Steve were arriving in two short days, and she needed to save the drama, so to speak, for her mama. She had linens to launder, pillows to fluff, dust bunnies to banish, and some nasty-ass baseboards to scrub—thankfully, Jenna had committed to helping her (in part, Rell suspected, to avoid dealing with Scott). But Rell needed to get a handle on herself as well, because not only would she soon have to discuss her plans for the summer with her mother, she would no doubt have to see Trevor, posing and smiling with Trina and his parents and probably hers too, like they were one big happy family.

Who should arrive the next morning in the midst of this blitz but Crockett, standing shirtless on their front steps, his biceps burnished brown by the sun. He smiled when Rell and Jenna appeared in the doorway. "Ladies," he said, "you're both looking exceptionally lovely today."

"To what do we owe?" Rell asked drily as he stepped inside.

"Just happened to be in the 'hood."

Of course you were, Rell wanted to tell him, you live three blocks away. But he was already pulling up a chair in their kitchen. Watching Crockett pour himself a cup of yerba maté, it occurred to her that there was something wrong about his Lion of Judah tattoo. Was it the way the lion was holding the Ethiopian flag? Did it seem to suggest, perhaps, the presence of opposable thumbs? And those dreadlocks, if you could call them that—those were new. If this guy really was undercover as a Deep Canyon student, he had definitely nailed a certain type of first-year wannabe rasta. Crockett actually made Trevor—with his perfect, Jewish dreads and laid-back, perpetually stoned vibe—look like the real thing.

Crockett must have sensed her attention, because he said, "Hey, by the way, Rell, great preso."

Rell blinked. Preso?

"Baccalaureate. I dug what you were saying about the morphology of the ponderosa pine being a function of its environment. That must have been pretty rad to study."

Baccalaureate was an event largely aimed at substantiating for East Coast parents why they'd pissed away tens of thousands of dollars on a little school out West no one had ever heard of—but it was, nevertheless, kind of a big deal. Of course, her mom and Steve had good reasons for why they'd had to miss it (the airfare being more expensive, not being able to get the time off, a new job, etc.), but that didn't lessen the sting of it, necessarily. Which made the fact that Crockett had not only gone to see her presentation but remembered specific details of it all the more charming.

"It was pretty rad," Rell said, warming to her subject. "Just the way some of these seeds are built is wild. To withstand these extreme temperatures during fires and then sprout months later like nothing happened—"

But Crockett's eyes were locked on Jenna's, and Jenna's were locked on his.

"—kind of blows your mind."

"Seriously," he said.

"How's Katie?" Jenna asked.

Crockett dropped his gaze to the table. "Let's just say, things have been rough between us lately." He ran a fingernail along a scar in the wood of the old tabletop. "She's an incredible person. I've never met anyone like her. I wish..." He cleared his throat. "It just seems like we're headed in different directions right now."

"Jeez," Jenna said. "I can totally relate. It's like me and Scott just want different things."

Slowly, with a drama indicative of great personal suffering, Crockett looked up. "Wow," he said. "It sounds like we're really going through the same thing."

Rell could not help but roll her eyes. And yet, you almost had to respect Crockett's bullshit, the sheer efficacy of it.

He leaned across the table and glanced at each of them in turn. "Honestly," he said, "I'd appreciate it if you kept an eye on Katie for the next couple days."

Jenna went still at that, and Crockett's gaze fell back to the table.

"You didn't," Jenna said.

"Didn't what?" Frankly, Rell was getting tired of being the last to know.

They turned to her in unison, looking like two kids caught in the act of setting the shed on fire. Then they turned back to each other, and Jenna stood. "I can't believe you!" she said. "Did you even think about me? Or Scott?"

"I thought you were trying to break up with Scott!"

"Well, yeah," Jenna said, "but not like this!" Her voice had jumped an octave; apparently, when Jenna was pissed, she sounded like a chipmunk. "Christ on a crutch, Crockett, what am I supposed to tell him now?"

"I'm sorry, okay? Things were just getting out of hand. It seemed like the easiest way for everyone. But Katie didn't take it the way I was expecting." Crockett looked off into the depths of the table, into the Rorschach of its wood grain, the countless liquids that had spilled there over the years and left their indelible mark. "I don't actually know what I was expecting, because I've never had a serious girlfriend before. It just seems like she's taking it hard." He looked up. "I mean, I am too, but…" He heaved a sigh and pushed his hair back from his forehead, like an actor on a daytime soap, but then stopped—clearly, he'd forgotten that he could no longer run his fingers through his hair. "I'm kind of worried about Katie right now."

That makes two of us, Rell thought.

Jenna's hand had flown to her mouth. "You don't think she might try to…?"

And for some reason here, Crockett glanced at Rell. "Honestly," he said, again, "I have no idea. Katie just seems like a loose cannon right now, and I wouldn't want her to do anything she'd regret. Maybe, if you talk to her mom, you could just tell her…"

"Tell her what?" Rell shared a look with Jenna.

Crockett shook his head. As if doing so would loosen the tangled mess he'd made of it. "Honestly, I don't know. I just don't want Katie to get into any kind of trouble she can't get out of."

Honestly, there was something about a person using the word *honestly* three times in as many minutes that made Rell think he was lying. And yet, as usual with Crockett, there was also something about this little performance that seemed sincere.

The doorbell chimed, which Rell took as an opportunity to excuse herself.

"Oh, hey, Rell." Squeaky clean and sweetly square in his chinos and Nikes, Scott was standing on their front steps with a dozen red roses and a bottle of sparkling cider. "Is Jenna home?"

Rell stepped out onto the front stoop, pulling the door half-shut behind her. "Hey, Scott," she said. "How's the EMT training going?"

"Good," he said. "I'm actually done. Still got my boards, though."

"That makes two of us! Not with the boards, but, like, graduating. Sort of. You've probably got a job all lined up." Rell laughed. Even to her, it sounded false.

Scott seemed unsure of how to respond. But then Jenna's and Crockett's voices erupted from the kitchen, cutting short any further subterfuge on Rell's part.

Scott, as he stepped into the kitchen—it positively killed her, the way the words died on his lips, the expression on his face when he saw Crockett sitting there at Jenna's breakfast table. Crockett, shirtless, caught in the act of pouring himself a mug of yerba maté, as if he owned the place.

"Scott," said Crockett. "Care for a cup?"

Scott just stood there, staring, first at Crockett, then at Jenna. His expression, his white-knuckled grip on the neck of that fogged bottle of Martinelli's—Rell knew what he was feeling, what he was thinking, the hot and cold flashes of anger and indignation. Remembering the way she'd felt the day she'd returned from winter break, calling Trevor's name, only to discover widespread evidence—he hadn't even bothered to hide it—that his new love bunny had taken up residence *in her house.*

Listen, she wanted to tell Scott, this isn't what it looks like. But then she saw the look on Jenna's face and reconsidered. Maybe Rell hadn't caught two kids about to set the shed on fire. Maybe they had already burned it down to the ground.

"Hey darlin'," Jenna said, rising. "Hey."

"Five years," Scott said to her. He turned to Crockett. "Five years."

Crockett nodded slowly, as if this phrase held some deep personal significance for him as well.

Scott turned to Rell, apparently trying to get a witness. "Five years," he said again.

"Five years," she repeated dutifully.

"Since sophomore year."

Tears had welled up in Jenna's eyes, and one of them slipped down her cheek. Scott watched as it dripped onto that heinous linoleum. He turned back to Rell.

"Since before 9/11," he told her. "Since…frickin' Clinton."

"Damn," she said.

"Five years." Gently, Scott set the cider and roses on the table between Jenna and Crockett. "Five years today."

Scott walked past them, through the kitchen to the back door. He opened it, but then he just stood there, like he was trying to think of something to say. What could he, really? Jenna was his high school sweetheart. He'd moved across the country for her. He'd helped her and her roommates break up and turn over twenty cubic yards of rock-hard, high-desert dirt—helped them fertilize it and plant it with tomatoes and peppers and melons that were, even now, out there dying in the sun. He'd been the good guy at every turn, and where had it gotten him?

All at once, Scott set off running, chinos and all, across the porch, through the backyard, past the garden beds, and out into the alley out back. Jenna ran after him, calling his name.

Rell half expected Crockett to follow suit, at least insofar as getting the hell out. But there he sat at her kitchen table, like the coyote who'd caught the cat, staring at the scar in the wood—who knows where it had come from—smoothing his goatee. When silence finally descended over the house, Crockett lifted his gaze to hers. "I know what you're thinking," he said.

Rell ran the tip of her tongue along her top teeth. "Honestly," she said, "I'm not sure you do."

"You're thinking I was just saying all that about Katie to get back with Jenna."

This sudden candor was refreshing. Still, Rell could not help but point out that as far as she knew, he'd never actually been with Jenna.

"Right." He held her eye. "But you know what I'm saying. I just wanted you to know. I'm not making anything up. About Katie."

And for once, Crockett appeared totally guileless, humorless, full on bullshitless.

It made him seem like a whole different person.

* * *

That night, for the first time in months, Rell dreamed of Trevor, the same dream that she'd been so relieved to get free of. Walking in the door of her house—her new house in the barrio, which was also her old house in Bridal Creek—she discovered those telltale signs: the muddy paw prints, the stuffing ripped loose from the sofa, the scat in front of the fireplace. Then, horribly—it was still horrible, even though she knew it was coming—the mangled, lifeless body of Mr. Biggles, the crazy orange tabby she and Trevor had adopted, which Trevor had insisted remain with him. No matter how many times Rell had this dream, it still broke her heart, in a way that thoughts of Trevor no longer did: the sad sight of Mr. Biggles, his soft fur sticky with blood.

Usually, this was where she woke up. But this time Rell realized that whatever predator had trespassed against her was still at large, rustling around upstairs. Her first impulse was to run, but instead she found herself moving toward the sound, following it up the stairs to the landing. She stood before Katie's room. Slowly, the door swung loose.

Rell awoke to an imagined thump. Or what she was almost sure was an imagined thump, lying in bed in the dark, her heart racing, but then, a moment later, was not at all sure she had imagined. She listened hard, her senses on end—prickled, like fur—and heard the front door click quietly shut.

Had she locked it before bed?

Had Jenna?

No use lying awake in the dark, freaking herself out. Rell rose and walked to the landing, just as in her dream, and then to the threshold of Katie's door. She hit the light switch.

There were the show flyers, the old homework assignments, the clothes in disarray, the paintings, the same Indian bedspread on the wall. But when Rell cracked the door to Katie's closet, it was bare: no plastic sheeting, no card table. No batteries, wire, or kitchen timers.

She walked back into Katie's room and stood there under the harsh overhead fluorescent. In its light, Katie's paintings were even more discordant than they appeared by day, great garish splashes of color broken by muddy blacks and browns. But taken together, they had a kind of rhythm to them, an unexpected logic. One piece in particular struck Rell: There was a baleful red spot near the top of the canvas, nearly subsumed by darker hues. It was the apocalyptic red of a hot-season sun, shining through a sky choked with smoke, but darker, as if seen from underwater. There was something both ugly and beautiful about it. Some kind of light, trying to break through.

Could Rell fall asleep after that? Hell no, she couldn't fall asleep after that. The days were getting hotter anyway. Better to roll herself a cigarette, steep a cup of chamomile, and sit out on the back porch in the cool of the night imagining danger behind every shifting shadow, every nocturnal denizen of the barrio on the move: the gang of raccoons on the make, checking for open windows on the cars parked the length of the alley; the b-boys strolling home from the party down the street, from which could be heard a bass beat still faintly bumping.

Katie and Crockett, Crockett and Katie—but who was the fuel, and who was the fire? Strange, the way Katie hadn't even seemed surprised that someone from the FBI had called for her, had asked for her by name. But the girl sure had been rocked when Rell brought up Crockett, and Jenna too. The reason for that seemed obvious in retrospect, just the way Trevor's thing with Trina now seemed obvious. Clearly, certain types of obvious were not Rell's strong suit.

Scott's face came back to her, round and freckled, his pink nose perpetually sunburned. Poor guy. He really wasn't made for this place. He'd never get that golden-brown tan that Crockett had, never have that hustler's charm; he'd never be the guy who got the girl until he met a girl who deserved him.

And when it came down to it, wasn't it the same with her and Trevor? Trevor was cool, in an emotionally stunted sort of way. Rell had wanted that cool, because she wasn't. But she'd done all the work in that relationship—clung to it, even in the face of the obvious.

She couldn't help but remember the way Crockett had dropped that comment about Katie's mom. Like, of course, Rell talked to her all the time—like she had a direct line to the woman's office. What if Jenna was right about him? What if his goal at Deep Canyon—first with Jenna and then with Rell—had always been to get close to Katie, to entrap her? And maybe even send her over the edge by cheating on her with Jenna?

If he succeeded—if Katie succeeded in setting some fires with electrical timers, as the title of that manual suggested—Jenna was right: It would hit the news. It would impact the career of an embattled middle-of-the-road Democrat in a swing state and, undoubtedly, their entire school. Deep Canyon College would be pegged as a breeding ground for domestic terrorists.

In a way, it was crazy to consider that any shadowy power—be it the FBI, CIA, Department of Homeland Security, or some as-yet-unknown right-wing cabal—would go to such great lengths to accomplish such modest aims. And yet, the Black Cat really had been raided by the FBI that fall. Dyson Lathe really had taken his own life, just that past weekend, rather than be taken in. There really were undercover agents enrolled in classes that semester. And there really were people who considered environmental organizations like Greenpeace on par with Al-Qaeda, just like there really were people who'd been rounded up by the U.S. government and held captive for years now without anything approaching due process.

Such a climate could not help but fuel paranoia, and that's what seemed surreal—that Rell was actually living in a time when this kind of paranoia did not seem paranoid.

As the dark of night turned blue and then began to pale, Rell found herself returning to Crockett, the day he'd strolled into their backyard with that ridiculous goat in tow—and then that night at the German Jen. That morning at their kitchen table, obviously lying about something, even as he was telling the truth.

Who was he, really? And what kind of game was he playing?

Six

Raleigh for the Cause

PRETTY MUCH JUST AS SOON AS RELL managed to kiss the edge of sleep, she was awakened by a knock on her bedroom door. She'd been dreaming this time about the bagel shop.

"Rell, wake up." The voice was Jenna's. "Crockett's here. He said Katie stole his truck."

"Who?" Something about the revolving trays of the bagel oven breaking—Rell had ridden with a batch of everything to some highly unlikely alternate dimension at the bottom of the oven. Which was also Pittsburgh.

"Katie," Jenna told her. "Seriously, are you awake? Katie stole Crockett's truck. He didn't say it, but it sounds like he thinks she might be..."

Against her better judgment, Rell propped herself up in bed. "Might be what?"

Jenna blinked. "I don't know. Suicidal, maybe?"

Rell lay back down in bed. "Has it occurred to you," she said, "this might just be some kind of bullshit drama between the two of them?"

"Sure. I mean, definitely. But Rell—" Jenna lowered her voice. "What if he's right?"

Rell opened her eyes wide in an effort to convince herself that she was awake. In the same moment, she recalled Katie's closet from the night before. "Hold up," she said. "Let me get dressed."

Now they were sitting with Crockett around the kitchen table, once again, with a French press of yerba maté. Rell blew the steam off her cup. "Help me out with this," she said. "How can you say Katie stole your truck when you gave her the key?"

Crockett looked as bleary as she felt, with sleep at the corners of his eyes and yesterday's T-shirt on backward. He scratched at the tag by his neck. "Maybe she didn't steal it, exactly. But she borrowed it unexpectedly. I'm worried—"

"You're worried?" Foggy as she was—exhausted, really—Rell was tired of this whiny ringtone of his, this plaintive refrain. "We've hardly seen Katie since she started dating you. She doesn't answer her phone, she only shows up late at night, and the only thing she ever wants to talk about is the Wind Valley Pipeline. Jenna says Katie didn't even bother to go to finals, and this weekend, guess what? Some dude from the FBI called for her. Never mind that little project in her closet."

Crockett glanced over at Jenna and then back at Rell. For once, Jenna set her mouth in a hard line when he looked her way. It's as if she was finally able to recall in his presence the sorts of things she said about him behind his back.

"Crockett," Rell said, "what was Katie building up there?"

Crockett sat back and pressed his lips between his teeth.

"You set her up, didn't you?" That was Jenna's little chipmunk, rising, at last, to the occasion. She stood up from the table. "You used me to get to her, to get her to do this. You used me to break that poor girl's heart!"

"I didn't use you to do anything!"

"And now you want witnesses. You want us to go see whatever it is you set her up to do." Jenna's face was flushed, her head cocked. All that saccharine Southern sweetness was gone.

"I didn't set her up," Crockett insisted. "This whole thing was Katie's idea."

"Oh, come on," Rell said. Her mug of tea was growing cold, but she didn't care. "It's clear that Katie's got plans to set something on fire, and we all know how obsessed she is with the Greene River. It doesn't take a genius to figure out that she's going to monkey wrench the pipeline—it's the same thing you always talk about, but she's actually going to do it. And you're going to sit here and tell us you had nothing to do with it?"

Crockett pressed the heel of his hand into his eye. "It's not—I mean, yeah, at first." He looked up at Jenna. "That's why I told her. I thought if we broke up, she wouldn't go through with it."

Jenna was having none of it. "Crockett, you are lying like a rug—like a dog—like a dog on a rug!"

"Listen." Crockett stood, finally, wide-eyed, now fully frazzled. "I'm sorry, okay? I've made some serious mistakes, and I feel like shit right now. Not that either of you care. Which is fine. If I were you, I wouldn't care either. But I'm not you, and I'll feel even shittier if I don't get out to Wind Valley before Katie goes through with this, and I don't have any way to do that right now, because *I don't have my truck.*"

Jenna looked to Rell. Rell shrugged. At this point, they were running a risk whether they went with him or not.

Crockett angled behind her to get a look at the clock. "We have an hour," he told them, "tops."

"Fine." Rell stood. "Get in the car."

The Vulva really was not capable of peeling out. But had it been, they totally would have, because that's how hardcore they were, trailing their phantom roommate/girlfriend past Ransom Row and the courthouse plaza, past the Chili Chuckwagon and on to Big Box Land, to Goldwater Highway and then down the long, dusty straightaway of Wind Valley Road. Fifteen minutes later, they passed the little cluster of houses around the Safeway that served as the ranching community's city center and emerged into the dry yellow grasslands—punctuated here and there by scrub oak or pinyon—that stretched from Wind Valley north to Ash Fork and the Grand Canyon beyond.

Crockett was sitting in the passenger seat beside Rell, leaning against the door, watching the hills in the distance roll by. He'd seemed genuine back there in the kitchen, but now that they were in the car with him, letting him direct them to some unknown location way the hell out in the wind-battered cattlelands of northern AZ, Rell found herself returning to the conversation she'd had the day before with Jenna.

"So, Crockett," Rell said, "where did you grow up again?"

"Audacious, Nebraska." He didn't bother to look at her as he said it.

"Funny," Jenna chimed in from the backseat, "I looked it up. There's no such place."

"Not anymore. It hasn't been a town since 1936. My folks just have a farm in the area."

"I thought it was a ranch," Rell said, and in the mirror, Jenna smiled.

"It was a farm first and then a ranch. My dad got—"

"Screwed over in the nineties by NAFTA." Jenna said it for him. "And then moved into cattle. Grassfed. Like there was even a market for grassfed beef back then."

Before he could respond, Rell piled on. "How about chickens? Did your folks have chickens when you were growing up?"

"What?" Crockett cast her a glance. "Sure."

"Did they let their chickens right range next to the road, the way you do? Did they let their goats out to visit the neighbors?"

Crockett was looking at her now like she'd lost her mind. Which only seemed to embolden Jenna. She leaned between the two front seats and said, "And hey, I've been wondering, what kind of tractor did you have, growing up?"

"A Deere."

"Compact or utility?"

"How would I know?"

"What, you didn't get to drive it?"

"Also," Rell said, "did your folks happen to grow weed on this farm/ranch thing? Because that bong on your bookshelf is probably worth more than this car."

"Look," Crockett said, "it's here. Take a right."

They hung a right down Bonner Road and were soon rolling past that long parcel of land Rell had studied so many times on maps—the ranch that belonged to the Giffords, the last of the landowners who'd stood between the City of Crest Top and the aquifer that fed the Greene. The Giffords had held out the longest, but in the end they'd taken the money from Blain, despite the efforts of Vern Bonner, their neighbor to the east, to broker a deal with the Central Arizona Water Alliance. The Wind Valley Pipeline route, Rell knew, ran right through this ranch.

"It's just a little farther," Crockett said. "Up here and to the—"

"Oh my god!" Jenna ducked down in her seat.

"What?" Rell looked around, but she found nothing more noteworthy than the dust rising behind a lone ATV over the hill to their right.

"It's Scott," Crockett said mater-of-factly. "He's out here jogging. What a dude."

"What do you mean by that?" Jenna asked from atop the trash on the floor mats in the back where she was crouching.

"I mean, the guy is fit as shit. Did he run all the way out here?"

"No, he probably parked along Wind Valley Road. He likes to—"

"He already saw you, by the way."

Rell searched the rearview mirror. Sure enough, there was Scott, running by the side of the road in his little red jogging shorts and charity-run shirt, which said *Raleigh for the Cause.* He seemed to have gotten a reading on them, because when she slowed and turned right at Crockett's behest, Scott turned right too. She checked the passenger-side mirror: there he was, pounding the ground behind them.

"Is there a reason your ex-boyfriend would be following us?" Rell asked.

Crouched amongst the layers of late-night takeout wrappers and handouts for classes long past, Jenna looked both silly and sad. "He's not exactly my ex." She cast a glance up at Crockett. "Yet."

Rell could not help but stare at her in the rearview mirror. Scott had taken Jenna back? After all that? And she'd let him?

"I know! It's terrible. I just wanted a chance to end it on a better note."

Rell looked over at Crockett, sitting there beside her, searching the landscape up ahead. *Hell*, she thought, *these two deserve each other.*

"I think I might have told him I was on some kind of end-of-semester field trip," Jenna said.

"Field trip to where?" Rell wanted to know.

"I don't know! Gray's Farm or something. Scott keeps wanting to have this big talk." Jenna clambered back up onto the seat, bouncing awkwardly as they hit a section of exposed bedrock. "I think." She cleared her throat. "I think he's actually planning to propose."

"Oh no," said Rell.

"Oh yes," said Jenna. "And now he's probably seen Crockett too."

"Slow down," Crockett said. "Here's the turn off."

The old ranch road had given way abruptly to a jeep trail, and up ahead, on the sturdy sandstone shelf beside the arroyo to their right, sat two rows of bulldozers and heavy-duty excavators. This was the same minor army, Rell realized, she'd seen that spring lined up down Goldwater Highway. There was no logical reason for them to be here: The pipeline route ran due west, the way they'd come, through the middle of the

Giffords ranch. What's more, the pipeline project was on hold until the judge settled Vern Bonner's water rights claim, that last-ditch Hail Mary to save the Greene.

Those rigs were just stationed out here, facing the Bonner Ranch, to intimidate him. Like the explosions that had destroyed the old man's cow tanks, like the grassfires that had burned across those fifty or so acres of his ranch that spring.

As the trail climbed a rise, the sandstone shelf gave way to a basalt ridge, at the base of which they found Crockett's 4Runner. Rell parked the Vulva beside it, and they all piled out. At first it seemed like Crockett was more interested in the condition of his truck than he was in the whereabouts of their estranged roommate—but no, he was just checking the back. Which was empty, aside from a number of red plastic gas cans.

Rell said, "Are those—"

"Empty." He lifted his chin toward the ridge. "Over there."

One by one, they scaled the ridge. One by one, they saw it: a smaller collection of yellow excavators—ten or so lined up together, plus one parked off by itself to the north—had been driven down through the arroyo and up the other side. Technically, they were probably over the property line, parked on the Bonner Ranch. As Rell watched, a figure who could only have been Katie, her green half-hawk pulled back in a practical pony, dressed in desert camo, emerged from behind one of the rigs.

"Katie?" said Jenna.

"Fuckin' A," said Rell.

Crockett said nothing. He just started scrambling down the ridge.

Rell followed him but took her time. If she knew Katie, Katie would not be happy to see them, Jenna especially; best to let Crockett absorb the major damage. Jenna seemed to come to a similar conclusion, because she assumed an even slower pace, stopping now and then to turn back to the ridge behind them. Scanning, no doubt, for Scott.

There was a strong wind out of the west today, and the sight of it moving through the grasslands toward Angus Mountain, looming in the distance, gave Rell that feeling she remembered from when she'd first come West—the sense of being a small point of observation in a vast landscape possessed of deep history. The basalt ridge they were descending appeared to be part of a geological subduction—a section of rock quite old, no doubt, as such rocks in this part of the world often were, pushed up from below the last time the earth here had shifted and stretched and yawned, two million years or so ago, when Angus Mountain had formed. Rell reached the bottom of the ridge, crossed the broad, flat wash, and scaled the other side. As she did, it reappeared, that mountain, the northern end of the Piconcillos, its foothills green, like a great ship adrift in a dry sea. The wind moved in waves across the face of Wind Valley, its golden grasses rising up along the flanks of Angus and on to the Greene River Valley beyond.

Regardless of the reason, it felt good to be out here this morning, in the warm and wide-open wind, in the sun, where a person could see for a hundred miles. Rell had spent so long working on her senior thesis, stuck behind that little screen, she'd almost forgotten what it felt like to be in places like this, where the big picture always seemed clear.

But as slowly as she'd walked, considering all of this—considering the crumbling shale that cropped up here and there, where Blain's excavators were parked, the delicate basket of a cactus skeleton—it seemed she'd arrived too soon.

"How else was I supposed to get here?" Crockett was saying.

"Well, you didn't have to bring *her.*" Katie practically hissed it.

Rell cast a glance back at Jenna, who managed to look both sheepish and indignant. As if now that she'd convinced Rell to drive them out to this place, she had no idea why they were here.

"How long?" Crockett asked.

"You were all about it. Then it was all, 'I don't know' and 'it's risky' and 'we have to be sure.' Mr. Black Bloc, 'I was in Seattle in '99.'"

"I *was* in Seattle in '99!"

"Visiting your grandma, maybe. You were, like, fifteen." Katie shook her head. "Jesus, Crockett. I can't believe I believed you."

"Katie, how long do we have?"

"Why should I tell you?"

"I'm just trying to—"

"What? Get me thrown in prison?"

Crockett's eyes were wide, his mouth slightly agape. He seemed to have reached some breaking point here. "Katie, I'm out here trying to save your ass, all right? Fuck. For fuck's sake. Because I fucking love you, all right? So sue me."

Katie's face contracted and then, after a long moment, crumpled. The way, Rell imagined, the Snoquomish Dam once had, giving way to all that pressure, all that water held back for so long. "You tell me that now?" Katie said. "After all this? After what you've been…" She choked, as if gagging on the words.

"Katie, you're amazing. You're the amazing person I wish I was, and that's the truth. But I can't do this anymore."

Katie's eyes were shut, her lips pressed together.

"I love you, all right? I've never said that to anyone before. But I'm an asshole." Crockett was staring down at the rock-hard desert dirt as he spoke. "If we stayed together, I'd only break your heart."

"Well, you're breaking it now."

Rell looked away. Overall, this seemed less like a setup than a breakup, a terribly messy one, the likes of which all three of them at 737 Sycamore seemed destined to endure that year.

They were standing beside that line of yellow excavators—Rell counted ten of them lined up nose to tail. Ten excavators parked on the Bonner Ranch, where no excavators should have been. Hadn't she counted ten kitchen timers in Katie's closet?

Rell turned back to her, expecting to find that same crumpled mess. But no, there was that studied intensity Rell had seen in Katie at the Black Cat. She said, "You're a liar, Crockett." Then again, loud enough to carry: "*Why* are you such a *liar*?"

"He *is* a liar!"

Scott had appeared on the ridge behind them. For a moment everyone was stunned into silence by the sight of Jenna's boyfriend, flushed red with exertion, making his way down the ridge toward them. The world was so quiet, aside from the whine of the wind, that Rell actually heard crickets.

"You think you're smart, don't you?" Scott said, his face red, two fingers pressed to a stitch in his side. He jogged another hundred yards down and then stopped again. "Stealing peoples' girlfriends and telling them all kinds of"—he appeared to be struggling for breath here—"crap? Well, guess again." Finally, he reached the bottom of the arroyo. Standing there, winded, he looked up at Jenna, wearing an expression so ominous that, on him, it was almost comical. "Field trip, my butt."

"Hey, babe." Jenna smiled down at him stupidly, like she was so happy to have run into him here, of all places.

"No!" he said. "Not this time! It's not like I don't know what you two have been doing."

Jenna, panicked, looked suddenly ten years younger. As if her teddy bear had dropped in the toilet. "Scott," she said, "I swear to god, we never did. Except that one time in the back of the bike shop, but other than that—"

"Jenna!" Scott said, his voice breaking like a squeaky clarinet.

Jenna, tearing up, turned away.

Scott sprinted the last few feet up the side of the arroyo to the spot where they stood, beside a hulking yellow excavator. He turned to Crockett. "You should be ashamed of yourself. Trying to pass yourself off as some kind of man of the land, farmer, cowboy—whatever it takes to get you laid, right, Justin?"

Crockett eyed Scott boldly. Crockett had five inches on him, at least. "Fuck you, Scott."

Scott hesitated only a moment. "Fuck you," he said, and Jenna almost choked.

"Whoa, slow down," Rell said. "Who's Justin?"

And now here, at last, Scott grinned. Here, at last, was the big speech he'd planned for the big occasion, and it wasn't the speech anyone had expected of him. "Justin Lynch," he said. "That's his real name. He's the son of Edward Lynch, the largest real estate developer in the state of Nebraska. Big oil man too. And you know what, Jenna?" Scott leaned in here to deliver the coup de grace. "Edward Lynch has *the* largest carbon footprint of *any* single human being on the face of the *earth.*"

Jenna's big blue eyes practically bugged out of her head. "Are you serious?"

"Totally serious." Then Scott seemed to focus on the blue shadow of Angus Mountain in the distance. "Well, there are a couple guys in Saudi, but when you calculate the total barrels of crude expended per day per guy times the amount of carbon released during the process of refining and shipping, plus the resources consumed by the average single-family home, yeah. For sure."

For the second time that semester, Rell's big ol' geeky heart gave a squeeze. But this time, she knew, she was not being played. Scott really was that geeky. Which was pretty much the point she decided, whatever it was they were actually doing out here, she was Team Scott all the way.

Katie turned back to Crockett. "What about seeing Rise Against in Omaha in 2001?"

Crockett was indignant. "I did see Rise Against in Omaha in 2001."

"Okay, then what about their lead singer convincing you to listen to Bob Marley?"

Crockett (Rell could not call him Justin) looked off at that. "All right, so maybe that was some bullshit. But I did get into Rastafarianism at a punk show."

No, Rell wanted to tell him, you got into smoking weed at a punk show. Then you went home and spent fifteen minutes on the Internet and got yourself that stupid tattoo. Come to think of it, was that lion of his actually waving the flag of Ethiopia? Or was that the flag of, like, Bolivia or something?

Katie looked suddenly stricken. "A trustafarian?" She turned to Rell. "I fell for a *trustafarian*?"

"Hey," Rell said, "join the club."

Jenna had her head cocked, listening; she turned to the excavator to her left, the closest in that long line that stretched beyond them for the next half mile or so.

All at once, their eyes met. All at once, Rell understood: that wasn't crickets she'd heard, it was a chorus of kitchen timers. "You guys," she said.

But now Crockett had turned to Scott. "Maybe you're right. Maybe I am a liar. Maybe I lied because I was insecure. Maybe I lied because I wanted to be judged for who I am instead of who my old man is. So fine. Call me a liar. You can even call me a pussy, though that's a highly sexist insult, because when it comes right down to it, I don't always have the courage to live the truth of my convictions. But you, Scott? You're a fucking weenie."

Scott was fuming now, his scalp showing pink through his hair.

Katie pulled out her cell phone and flipped it open. "Fifteen minutes," she said.

Jenna turned to Rell. Rell, the adult in the room. Once again, Rell said, "You guys, listen."

But Crockett wasn't listening to any of them. Because Crockett had also been waiting for this moment for quite some time. "Face it, dude—Jenna is a beautiful, brilliant, creative young woman, and there's no way in hell a guy like you would have wound up with her if you hadn't grown up together in the same little hick town in North Cackalacky or wherever the fuck you're from. What is it, like, five hundred people?"

"You'd better shut up right now," Scott told him.

"Or what?" Crockett stared him down.

"Hey," Jenna said, finally. "We have a—"

But then Scott hauled off and socked Crockett square in the face and Jenna screamed.

Crockett staggered back, clutching his nose. Then he rushed Scott headlong, tackling him to the ground. They fell to blows amid the gravel and bunch grass beside the closest bulldozer. Scott was smaller, but Crockett was right: dude was fit as shit. Even on his back, he held his own. When Crockett swung and missed, Scott flipped him over and pinned his skinny ass to the ground.

And now Katie was halfway up the ridge. "Katie!" Rell yelled. "Where are you going?"

Katie stood for moment, hands to her knees, catching her breath. "You assholes can stay out here as long as you want," she said. "But you're standing ten feet from a Class 3 felony, and in twelve minutes, this whole thing is going to blow."

Rell flashed back on the empty gas cans in the back of Crockett's truck. *How to Set Fires with Electrical Timers.* The dry yellow grasslands stretched out all around them. The wind out of the west, waving through it, all the way up to Angus Mountain and beyond.

"Katie!" All together, everyone turned to Rell. Everyone except for Katie, who stayed the course in her dogged climb up the basalt. "*This is not a joke!*" Rell wasn't sure she had ever screamed like this, at anyone, in such desperation. She could feel it in her body—not just the intensity it took to produce such a sound but the actual vibration of it in the air. The strange power of her voice.

"When those timers blow—"

"They'll set fire to a million dollars' worth of equipment," Katie said, "that belongs to Blain." She wasn't speaking loudly, but she didn't have to. The wind carried her voice down the ridge as surely as it would carry a spark east to the ponderosa forests of Angus Mountain. Katie checked her phone. "Eleven minutes."

Rell took a breath. It was as if all her years of study—all those days she'd spent at burn sites, collecting seeds and soil samples—all the hours she'd spent in the library, mapping the relationships between the weather patterns and plant communities of central Arizona—even the drowsing hours she'd spent trying to master the inanities of citation styles—had all led her here, to this moment. "When those electrical timers blow," she heard herself saying, in the same clearly enunciated tone she'd used at baccalaureate, pitched louder to compensate for the wind, "they'll throw off the kind of heat that causes chaparral to spontaneously combust."

Rell extended an arm, indicating the landscape, the great dry sweep of it before them. "You see that mountain over there? The wind is blowing straight across this stretch of ranchland to the foothills. If those timers blow, within hours, that whole forest will go up. And when it does, the topography here will create convection, carrying firebrands as far as the Greene Valley." She turned back to Katie. "This state is in a serious drought. If you lit that mountain on fire, you'd wind up burning a quarter of the state before anyone managed to put it out."

Katie's face was blank. "You said—"

"I said what?"

"It's just grassland out here. You said."

"What? When?"

"It would just burn toward the road."

The worst part about this was realizing that Katie had actually been listening to her that day. What other stupid notions had Rell inadvertently planted in her head? "A fire started by a couple sticks of dynamite, sure, half-drowned by an exploding cow tank, with a wind out of the east—but this wind's straight out of the west, probably fifteen miles an hour. Are you kidding me? If all of these rigs start to burn, this will be a war zone."

Katie just stood there on the ridge, staring. Not quite in disbelief, but what? It was the face of someone taking a curve too fast on a motorcycle, realizing that they were headed into a collision; the face of someone who'd jumped from a plane, only to discover the rip cord of their parachute was stuck. It was the face of someone realizing, for the first time, that the rest of her life would forever be defined by some dumb decision she'd made in her youth.

"Katie," Rell said, calmly, clearly, "*how do you disarm the timers?*"

Katie lifted one hand, and then she let it drop. Clearly, some kind of traffic jam was occurring in her brain.

"Katie," Rell said again.

Katie opened her mouth. But instead of speaking, she took two steps and disappeared over the ridge.

"Are you taking my truck?" Crockett yelled after her.

The only reply was the whine of the wind through the grass amid that chorus of kitchen timers tick, tick, ticking down the row. Crockett turned to Rell. "You have to rip off the wires without letting them touch, or they'll throw off a spark. But it's dangerous, and we don't have enough time."

"The hell we don't," Rell said. "Split up."

But they all just stood there looking at her. Crockett said, "Won't we get our fingerprints on them? I mean, I don't know about you, but if my folks found out…"

Scott cleared his throat. "I have my boards coming up."

Jenna said, "What if one of those timer things starts a fire before we can get to all of them, and then the police get here, and they see us with them, and they think—"

"Listen." Rell could feel the heat in her cheeks. She was scared but sure. She knew this landscape, in this season. And she knew herself—what she could live with and what she could not. "If you want to let that mountain burn, go ahead. If you want to let every home in Wind Valley go up in smoke, be my fucking guest. But I, for—"

And just like that, Scott had slid beneath the excavator beside them.

Rell sprinted to the next excavator down the line, and a moment later, she could hear Crockett and Jenna hustling to do the same.

Katie's incendiary device was little more than a dish tub filled with diesel, over which she'd suspended a structure supporting a kitchen timer augmented with a match and two wires attached to a battery and a road flare. But it was hard to get the wires free without touching them together and without spilling the diesel—the fumes under the excavator nearly knocked Rell out as she fumbled, sideways, trying to keep an eye on that timer: just over eight minutes. There was no way she could take this long on the next one.

Working quickly, her hands shaking, Rell was struck by a sort of euphoria. As ridiculous a thought as it may have been, she was actually doing something with her education. She had influenced people to take action, to do the right thing. Which, for once, was entirely clear.

By the time Rell was out from under excavator #2, Jenna had already dismantled the devices under #3 and #4, a few hundred yards down the line. "Don't bother with the wires," she told them, "just break off the match." Even as she spoke, Scott was sliding out from under excavator #5, moving past Crockett, whose legs were sprawled out under excavator #6. Working like this, quickly and methodically, running between the rigs, they formed a sort of leapfrog relay team, until at last all that terrible ticking ceased.

They walked to the front of the last four excavators. Slowly, they rotated in place. Silence. Nothing but the whirr of the wind and, far off, the white noise of traffic down Bonner Road.

"Look," Crockett said, one hand shielding his face from the sun. He was looking off toward the Giffords ranch, where a plume of dust was rising through the air.

"It's headed this way," Rell heard herself saying.

Suddenly, Jenna's capability in the face of crisis evaporated. She turned to Scott, as if Scott might have a magic wand or a teleportation device that—*poof!*—could get them out of this. But Scott, like Rell and Crockett, was tracking that line of dust moving toward them.

"It's too late," Scott said. "Whoever it is, they're going to come right over that hill and see Rell's car."

And just like that, all the euphoria Rell had felt in speaking those basic truths of climate and convection, in running from one great yellow excavator to the next, in scrabbling beneath them to dismantle Katie's timers, evaporated. Because of course that truck would stop when its driver saw her car parked at the base of that ridge. What reason did her car have to be there, in such close proximity to all this heavy equipment? On private property? The Vulva, plastered with her *Save the Greene!* and *Central Arizona Water Alliance* bumper stickers—with her Deep Canyon College parking permit clearly visible on the dash.

They could run, but where to? The Bonner house, Rell knew, was a good ten miles to the north, and Old Man Bonner's love for the Greene River aside, if he caught them trespassing, he'd be sure to exercise his Second Amendment rights. He'd said as much during an alliance meeting when a college student had suggested holding a vision council on his land.

The line of dust disappeared as the jeep trail curved around the bend—they could hear the sound of a motor now in the quiet that had fallen. Then a truck appeared atop the basalt ridge. It sat there for a moment, and then a man got out. Slowly, he walked to the edge of the ridge, his cowboy hat silhouetted against the sky.

"Jesus H.," said Rell.

"Holy jeez!" Jenna breathed.

"Well, I'll be," Crockett said softly. "If it isn't George Blain himself."

Despite the heat of the day, the sizzle of the sun, and what Rell was beginning to recognize, even now, as the first signs of heat stroke, she felt herself shiver.

And then, just as slowly, the figure in the hat took a step back. He turned to his truck, hopped up, and slammed the door shut. He reversed and drove off.

Crockett tilted his head like a dog. "You hear that?"

One by one, they turned and listened. Somewhere, a timer was still ticking.

"How?" Jenna asked.

That lone bulldozer Rell had spotted on her descent down the ridge—the one that stood alone, away from the others. She took a step toward the arroyo and spotted it, another quarter mile to the north at least. The others followed suit; they saw it too, but what could they do? Rell shut her eyes. It was too late, too far to stop that spark. The fire would be all but impossible to put out, given their available resources. She opened her mouth to say it but found herself stopped short.

Scott was airborne. With those skinny legs and broad shoulders, at rest he looked like some kind of startled stork. But when he ran, the boy was pure poetry. He was made for this, and he knew it: made to run, made to respond in the face of disaster. There he was, sprinting, crossing the distance—*Raleigh for the Cause!*—faster than anyone else could.

Scott slid in beside that last, lone excavator like he was sliding into home base, and a moment later he stepped out from behind the rig. Slowly, he turned and jogged back, and all three of them let loose with a cheer.

* * *

If the man in the cowboy hat was George Blain, maybe he had decided they weren't worth the trouble to confront. Maybe he hadn't wanted to risk them connecting him to those dynamite charges at the Bonner Ranch—where he, like all those big yellow excavators, had no good reason to be. Or maybe he'd just taken down Rell's license plate number and decided to watch and wait. Rell didn't know, but if she stuck around Crest Top, she had the feeling she was going to find out.

Though if he really was George Blain, that was the first she or anyone else she knew had actually seen of him; the man had never shown up at any of the public hearings surrounding the pipeline. His face had been in shadow, but that stance, that hat, the way he'd stood there looking down at them, as if both cocky and unsure—it was, oddly, as if the President of the United States had appeared there briefly on the ridge above them.

Katie's face, though—standing up there, she'd had that look of absolute certainty, followed by an expression Rell almost couldn't name. It was as if this catastrophic miscalculation on her part had removed, for her, any possibility of the world's redemption. She'd risked everything with this one reckless gesture and failed to change the world. Now she might as well just give up, go home, and embrace whatever fate she'd sought to dodge by moving West.

The way she'd turned and walked over the ridge that day—she looked like a soldier stepping out in front of a firing squad.

Maybe it was that kind of courage Crockett had fallen for, in his way. Crockett, the hustler, and Katie, the romantic; maybe the two of them, living under the shadows of powerful parents, really had fallen tragically in love. Rell remembered what Crockett had said: *Maybe I don't always have the courage to live the truth of my convictions.*

But Katie did. Or she had.

And yet, Rell wondered, was it courage that had led Dyson Lathe to set fire to those lumber mills, back in the day? To blow that famous dam? To take his own life when the law caught up with him? Or was it something else?

She was scrubbing the baseboards later that day, lost in thought, when the phone rang.

It was her mother. Who was due to arrive, Rell realized, in less than twenty-four hours. "Hey, how's it…" Rell had been about to ask if they were packed yet, but she trailed off, midsentence, feeling suddenly lightheaded.

"Sweetheart?" her mom said. "Are you all right?"

"I'm fine," Rell told her. Had she even drunk any water today? She caught a glimpse out the window at the temperature gauge on the neighbor's porch. It was ninety-eight degrees. At ten in the morning.

Her mom muffled the receiver and yelled something to Steve. "I just wanted to make sure I'm not missing anything. Is there anything you need from home?"

Slowly, Rell slid down the wall to the floor. "No, Mom. Just you."

Her mom was silent for a long moment. "You sound different, honey."

"I am different." Though what she meant by that, Rell could hardly say.

She could not help but think of Katie, walking home that morning after she'd hooked up with Crockett—Katie, in her sparkles and false eyelashes, smiling. So transparent, that girl had seemed, and yet it was clear now there was something about her that Rell had failed to see. Something maybe everyone had failed to.

"No, I mean just now. You sounded different. You sure you're all right?"

It occurred to Rell that maybe her version of her mother was no longer actually her mother, and her mother's version of her was no longer actually her. That maybe her own version of herself was no longer herself. That all these selves were turning into other selves, burning off in the heat of this strange summer, which had only just begun.

Seven

The Underground Waterfall

Michelle

THE PLAN HAD BEEN to take over the courthouse plaza with a daylong show of resistance that would draw state, maybe even national, news. But when temps reached the triple digits in the first week of June, organizers agreed that no press releases would be sent, no call to action announced. They could not ask people to stand outside in this heat, even beneath the shade of those benevolent elms that presided over the plaza—could not count on reporters from Phoenix being willing to leave the frosty confines of their offices to cover those few who would show. So the verdict arrived on June 15th without as much as a squeal of feedback from a bullhorn, without a single placard denouncing the pronouncement. The judge had struck down Vern Bonner's senior water rights claim on the Greene.

Michelle could not help but feel struck down herself, though it was only the latest in a series of blows. Hanging up the phone that day at the Cat, she felt them all, physically.

First the sucker punch, when Dyson had disappeared—how had Huckleberry known? Maybe he'd been in touch with old friends. Maybe he'd developed a sixth sense in his years on the road, on the run. Huck, the magic man, the one-man band, the one all the girls came around to see; Michele could not help but hate him now, though it wasn't his fault he was alive and Dyson was dead. Dyson, who'd slipped out without a word of warning, like a cat through an open window, the way she'd always known he would—that's what it was like, loving an outlaw. They'd fallen asleep together one night in December, and she'd woken up freezing, alone.

The second hit had been harder, strategically positioned: the raid on the Cat, and those dark days of interrogation. When had she cried like that, screamed, in such an unguarded way? In that room with the white walls—how far beneath the surface of the earth, who could say? Yet she'd come out of those days feeling galvanized, stronger in some way.

The third blow had come that spring, when those bruisers had shown up at the Cat, that polite knock at the back door. It was no more than a feint, that visit, compared to the news of Dyson's death that followed, a month later in Colorado. Somewhere west of Nederland, those bruisers had caught up with him; somewhere between Buckeye Mountain and Hurricane Hill, Dyson had taken that heavy little handgun of his, which he liked to think she didn't know about, and turned it on himself. That blow had been a direct hit, the uppercut that rattled her teeth, leaving them loose for days.

Now here at last was the hard left hook—the unraveling of everything to which they'd dedicated their lives these past six years. The cause that had meant the most to Dyson, the one closest to his heart. That river, which he'd given her. The great glittering stretch of the Greene.

And yet, it was the softest blow that had done the most damage. It was the names and ages of those girls, which they'd used to try to break her. They, the men in black and blue, bruisers, and Michelle had broken.

Sylvie, fifteen; Rachel, fourteen; and worst of all, Evangeline, just thirteen, back when Dyson was a freshman in college.

Now Michelle was sitting at the kitchen table trying to write his obituary for the *Earth Uprising Journal.* It was a task she'd been putting off for weeks, hoping to have something even marginally redeeming to say, following the day's verdict, and now that obit was overdue—the publication was waiting on her to go to press. And yet, instead of contemplating Dyson's legacy, she found herself studying the cellophane-faced gift box he had left on the shelf by the door, beside the dusty flowers of some long-ago hike and that leering Bob Dobbs bobblehead. Dyson had written on the box, in Sharpie, *In case of emergency, break glass.* Inside the box was a glass.

She'd come this close to following those instructions more than once since the boys in black and blue had left her bruised and battered. Because it would be satisfying, wouldn't it, to hear that glass shatter against the sidewalk?

Because those many shards severed so suddenly from one another, so unexpectedly, would look so fine under the fierce glare of the sun.

Because if she were to write these words on her own flesh, with what fine utensils she found there, they might hurt less than they did right now: Sylvie, fifteen; Rachel, fourteen; and Evangeline, just thirteen.

There was no sense in even trying to think in this heat, at this hour of the day, but she'd run them all off anyway: the peace group potluckers, anxiously awaiting the news, the high school heroes with their amplified fuzz on the back-porch stage, and even Roger, who practically lived at the Cat these days, out back by the creek, where he'd been turning a cottonwood stump into something you might call art. Day after day, he shaved those curls of wood away, revealing that particular female form, which must have been his thing: heavy hips, heavy tits. Not like Dyson, who seemed to have preferred skinny, boyish girls like her.

They'd shown her the pictures, those bruisers. Maybe just to make her see that she and those girls shared a body, a certain look. Not quite pissed, but stiff. As if they'd been surprised by something early on in life and never quite recovered.

And now here she sat in the heat of the day, alone in this place that was supposed to be a community center—alone in this place they'd built—with the summer's dust clogging her sinuses, hot tears in her eyes, trying to think of something, anything she could say about her husband at this point that did not feel like a lie.

Boyfriend, officially, because she'd been underage. Not that they were the kind of people who would have involved the state in any case. They were the kind of people who just decided what they were going to do and did it, for better or worse, till death did they part, and now they had, in fact, been parted.

She remembered the way they'd pulled over that day by the side of the road just south of Chinle, her first real taste of the Southwest. Up on the Navajo Nation, with the red rocks piled up around them like the landscape of a dream. Up on Diné, where skinny, frightened rez dogs roam and kiddies will show you dinosaur tracks for a quarter—where, at the time, Peabody Coal was sucking a billion gallons of pristine groundwater out of the desert each year to wash its coal slurry down to Laughlin. Seized by this urge to declare their love, that unbreakable bond, before those solemn stones.

It was a private ceremony, with just a few guests in attendance: that great horned owl, which they heard but never saw, and a few plucky, blue-bellied lizards. She and Dyson held hands, said their vows, and watched as a majestic golden eagle flew off with a half-eaten hamburger from the side of the road. And they'd laughed at that, but it wasn't a joke, exactly.

Or maybe it was.

Maybe she just hadn't known it at the time.

She'd been sixteen, Dyson forty. This was before she knew he was wanted by the FBI, or that Dyson was not his real name. Before September 11th and the so-called Patriot Act. Before a lot of things.

Before, for example, she could step foot in a big-box store without hyperventilating. Or walk through the meat department of a grocery. Her "condition," her mother called it—Dyson had understood that it was like an allergy for her. Michelle was allergic to society, its most toxic parts especially.

What pissed her off about those names and numbers, more than anything, was this: they reduced her to a number too. Because it didn't matter now, as far as anyone else was concerned, that she and Dyson had been serious about each other, and everything else, but they'd laughed like that, like kids. The way, in fact, she had no memory of actually laughing as a kid.

Her father always thought she did it for attention, hyperventilating in Walmart. Which was why he'd forced her to come whenever he made a trip. One time, she remembered, it was for toothpaste; another time, paper clips.

Mom took her aversions more seriously. Too seriously, after the zoo. *Aren't kids supposed to like the zoo?* her mother had asked the old family perv, Dr. Goorin. *There are certain children,* he told her, leering creepily at Michelle, *who prefer not to see the animals confined.* Certain children who'll scream and cry and pitch a fit when you drive past the moaning feedlot that smells like death and stretches clear to the horizon on the way to your sunny cottage on the coast.

Though Dr. Goorin never attempted anything more than placing his hot, heavy hand on her shoulder, she'd pleaded with her mother not to leave her alone with him. (Ironic, in retrospect, how sensitive she'd always been to that sort of thing.) Her mom had just shaken her head, the way she did, and delivered her father's line: *Michelle, don't be dramatic.*

Good people, her parents, but kind of dumb when it came to a kid like her. Who happened to be the only kind of kid they had.

First, it was Ritalin, because she never wanted to come in from recess. Then Xanax, because she started having panic attacks when they had to dissect frogs in junior high. Then there was Prozac, her old friend Prozac! Because she'd made the mistake of mentioning that sometimes, when she saw the bulldozers tearing out the woods where she'd played as a kid, it made her want to go to sleep and never wake up.

Dyson had a place like that, a patch of woods he'd called his own as a boy, though he'd always been careful not to mention where he'd grown up. At the time he'd said he was protecting her, and maybe he was—those bruisers had blustered and bullied her for days before they'd come to realize she knew nearly nothing about Dyson's life before they met. She didn't know, for instance, that he was born in Washington, just outside Spokane, or that he'd been an only child, like her. Unlike her, a good student. A track star, even.

Fitting, considering how much of his life he spent running.

According to the Federal Bureau of Investigation, Dyson had been "radicalized" by his years at Deep Canyon College and a subsequent stint in the Peace Corps. But Michelle wondered, what had sent him to Deep Canyon in the first place? The school's outdoor program, most likely. Because it takes one to know one, kid—Dyson was allergic to society too, though he'd held it together better than she did.

It was one of the first things they'd really talked about, how they'd both loved certain trees as kids. Outside of Spokane, she knew, there were a whole lot of trees—trees at the edges of everything man-made, and the man-made newer, flimsier, the way it was out West, the burbs still dwarfed by those vast tracts of wilderness upon which they were built. Where Michelle had grown up, smack dab in the heart of Ohio (which, as everyone knows, is *the heart of it all*), the burbs were being built on top of farms. Her housing development, once a hundred fertile acres or so, was home to no less than a thousand houses. Their tacky tract was in Phase III, on the edge of a subdivision known as Deer Run. Or, as she'd christened it, *Deer Ran.*

Michelle too had run, zigzagging across those five lanes of traffic—once a quaint country road—to reach that patch of woods. There were no crosswalks; the highway was meant for cars, not people, and certainly not children, who were apparently supposed to tool around on their bikes between all those ominously homogenous houses, the way they did in the fifties. But all the kids she knew had TV in their rooms and the latest gaming systems and pool parties, maybe, if their parents had sprung for a pool (useful in that climate just a few months of the year), which seemed the only context under which any of them ever played outside. Leaving kids like her, who got panicky and weird if they spent too much time indoors, to wander those fresh black streets like a ghost.

But on the other side of those five lanes, she'd found, was a forest—the back end of someone's back forty. And a spacious old maple, overlooking a creek. She'd told Dyson about it, how she used to sit beneath that tree. How sometimes a troop of turkeys or even a red fox would stroll right past, oblivious of her presence. They'd been camping that night on Mount Hood, just past Government Camp, with those big Doug firs spread out around them like a council of elders, listening. *That happens*, he said, *when you get to know a place. It stops being afraid of you.*

She'd told him about the morels and leeks and wild grapes she'd found in those woods back home. How sometimes she'd spend all day building a fort out of rotten logs and moss or launch a leaf or stick or feather she'd found down the creek and follow it as far as she could.

Which was how she'd discovered—deep in the tangled heart of that tangled mass of trees, enveloped in grapevine, there in *the heart of it all*—a place where the creek dropped through a hole in the forest floor. At the bottom of a ravine a thousand feet away she found a dark, wet passage, crumbling with clay, that led to a limestone cave.

The tunnel was narrow; only a child could have found it.

Inside the cave was a waterfall.

When they ripped up that maple, overlooking that creek—when they dammed that creek to make a pond—when they sent that red fox running and christened the place *Fox Hollow*—did the men who operated the equipment consider themselves terrorists? Did the ones who made the plans?

And really, which was the greater crime, destroying a dam or destroying a river?

Dyson. Even now, his name came to her like a great reprieve, like a stroke of the boldest luck, like a blessing, though the men in black and blue would have her believe otherwise. *No one in their right mind*, they'd said. But she imagined they were people like the kids in her subdivision, who had never felt the need to run across that five-lane highway, maybe never even wondered what lay on the other side—people who had never loved a place and been forced to watch it die.

None of which would ever fit in an obit. Why, she wondered, had the Uprising even asked her to write it, when so many of Dyson's oldest friends were still part of that crew? She'd been sitting here in the heat with this spiral-bound notebook and ballpoint pen for what felt like days, unable to eat or drink, almost paralyzed. All she'd managed, so far, was his name: *Christopher Mason.*

Which wasn't even his name, as far as she was concerned.

She looked up at the box he'd left on the shelf by the door. It was still sitting there, that glass, in case of emergency. Waiting for her, the girl who'd broken, to break it. To write what she wanted to—their names—in bright angles on her skin. To break that thin, soft barrier that kept everything inside her from rushing out and everything outside from rushing in.

Though really, maybe she should just walk down to the liquor store on Cooper Canyon Road, the way she'd seen herself doing for days now, and pick up a fifth. She could walk back and fill that glass with whiskey and then drink it down and fill it up again.

Until everything inside her shattered into sparks.

Until the immense weight of this paralysis had shifted, lifted.

That would be another, maybe a better way of breaking.

That's it? she could hear his voice saying. *You're not even going to put up a fight?*

She took her head in her hands, as if doing so could rid it of him. Because really, what right did he have? Her old man, goddamn—what kind of fight had he put up when they'd come for him?

Because she wanted it then, the way she hadn't in years: the burn of liquor on the back of her throat, the way it would numb her out.

Because she knew she would not be able to stop until she woke up at this very table tomorrow morning with this spiral-ring notebook pressed to the side of her face, wanting nothing more than to do it all over again.

Hold on to your anger. Don't let it turn to despair.

What do you know about despair? she asked him, his ghost, hanging like smoke in the air. His handwriting on the carefully labeled spices on the shelf beside the stove; his picture on the fridge, from the pipeline protest; his shoes by the back-porch steps. Despair was going on living when the one person who ever understood you was dead. That's what fucking despair was.

Fuck Dyson, Christopher, whoever. Fuck him for saving her life and taking his own. Fuck him for those other girls he'd fucked, those girls who'd looked like her. And fuck him, most of all, for being her friend.

Michelle had not had a whole lot of friends back in Ohio, but she'd been pretty tight with a guy named Kurt Vonnegut, who'd written a book called *Slaughterhouse Five.* In this book, whenever something terrible happened, the narrator, Billy Pilgrim, just said, *So it goes.*

She had her own version of it, which involved Sydney, the blue-and-orange tokay gecko who'd been held captive in the back of her third-grade classroom, who died the winter the electricity failed and the heat went out. Every morning of her freshman year, she looked out at the new development going up on the other side of the highway and said to herself, *So much for Sydney.*

And laugh, but it wasn't a joke.

It came back to her, that line, staring at Dyson's shoes, those ratty old Vans with the holes in the soles. She'd thrown them out three times, at least, and every time found them right back at the door. Dyson had told her those shoes were a family heirloom, that they were lucky, that they scared off demons, the way gargoyles did. He'd told her all kinds of lies about those shoes that were also true, and though she'd lived with those old Vans for years, she'd never learned the truth about them, any more than she had about him.

So much for Sydney.

Michelle could see herself getting up, walking to that door. Raiding the kitchen tip jar and then walking along the bike trail to Crook Street and from there up Cooper Canyon. It would make her feel better, wouldn't it, to get some exercise?

And as long as she was breaking, why not go all the way? Why not look up her old friend Crystal? Christina, Chris, Christy—whatever you called her, she and Jack made a fine couple. In fact, Michelle had found (when? sophomore year?) when used in the proper proportion, they leveled her out to a place where she would not have given two shits if her hair was on fire. Really, she was a lot more functional that way.

That too was something Dyson had understood, her need for medication. *Your pain,* he'd told her, *is a healthy reaction to a sick society. It's how you know you're alive.*

He was full of fortune-cookie wisdom, her old man. She could still see the way he'd shake his head and say, *Certain species don't fare well in captivity.* She'd thought he was talking about her, but of course he'd been talking about himself. Warning her, maybe, what he'd do if they tried to take him.

She was hit then by a memory—a flash, really—of the elementary school across the street from her old drug counselor. Squat, industrial, and nearly windowless, it was surrounded by a six-foot hurricane fence topped with barbed wire, just like her high school. Probably to keep drug dealers out—signs announced it was a *Drug-Free School Zone*—but from where she sat in her counselor's office, it looked like it was there to keep the kids confined there from attempting to escape.

And oh, the sloppy heartbreak on her mother's face, huddled close to Dad in that office, red-faced and snuffling, pleading, "Honey, didn't we teach you about drugs?" That familiar Prilosec bag she used for grading papers still slung across her shoulder.

Michelle thought of the way her mother always nagged her about taking her meds every morning. Like if Michelle didn't, she would just self-destruct before three o'clock. The way her dad washed his pills down with Pabst every night after work, like it was perfectly normal to keep working, well into your sixties, at a job that required prescription painkillers. And Michelle laughed, that numbed-out Prozac laugh. Until her father reached over and slapped her so hard she hit the floor and her drug counselor kicked him out of his office.

So much for Sydney.

Around the time Fox Hollow had gone up, food had become problematic for Michelle. She had already been hospitalized for anorexia, so when she got busted for speed, the next logical step was rehab. She didn't trust her parents at all at that point; they didn't trust her either, and in this, both parties were probably justified. So she sold off a bottle of her dad's Darvocets to some freshmen ravers she knew, hopped a Greyhound, and dropped out of school.

What had she known about the great state of Oregon except that it had trees? Which wasn't even really the case east of the Cascades. Her plan, if you could call it that, was to go live in the National Forest, where she could forage nuts and berries or maybe grow weed and sell it to hippies, which she'd heard was a thing you could do. Her concept of camping was pretty sketchy at that point, but like a lot of things, she figured she'd figure it out when she got there.

All kinds of kids like her were pouring into Portland then—caught up, she'd often thought, in the wake of Kurt Cobain, following him the same way down. Heroin was big in those days and easy to come by, and in this, as in so many ways, Michelle had been no more than lucky. She didn't have any money—or any friends generous enough to get her hooked—and she was too skinny to succeed in selling her ass the one time she'd actually tried.

Though they were her friends, those guys, and maybe the first real ones she'd had—Scum especially, whom she'd met not long after arriving in the City of Roses. Which smelled a lot more like piss than it did like roses, at least in Old Town by the bus station.

It had been a couple days since she'd landed, but she'd been wandering around with her backpack for what felt like a year. Getting on toward dark—she could still feel that panic, the way it came on in her first few days in the city at the first sign of dusk. She'd been trying to work out her plan for the night when she'd stumbled on that crowd outside the Roseland.

College hippies drinking brown-bagged beer and nappy tour kids enveloped in a cloud of ganja—she was familiar with this sort of scene from the parking lots of Akoustic Hookah shows back home. It occurred to her that these were the kind of people who might want to lift her spirits by kicking her down some sort of buzz.

But this being Portland, there was also a third group of people, unfamiliar to her then, who clearly had the same idea. These folks looked a little like members of the first two groups, but upon closer inspection, it was easy to tell the difference. College hippies had long hair; tour kids had dreadlocks; these folks had slept-on chunks of matted hair or crusty Mohawks caked with spray-paint. They were all defiantly dirty, and many of them wore black; one guy had facial tattoos, the first Michelle had ever seen.

The tour kids seemed aware of these people only as a kind of parasitic life-form on the organism of their scene; they would not give them the time of day, much less an American Spirit. But the college hippies could not tell the difference between these people and the tour kids, whom they wanted to impress, so they were forthcoming, she noticed, with nearly anything.

Then along came that lady, tottering toward them in the sort of bustier that was fashionable at the time—she must have been headed to one of the clubs in Chinatown. Her miniskirt kept riding up, and she kept tugging it down; every inch of her body was cinched and pinched in a way that was almost painful to see; everything about her seemed hesitant, unsure.

But when she noticed the riffraff outside the Roseland, her manner changed. The lady tossed her hair and assumed a runway stride; she averted her eyes, checked her manicure. It was like she was suddenly in some sort of movie—a movie that would never in a million years include people like them.

Michelle was standing next to the guy with the tattoos. The tattoos were a series of drawn-on stitches that followed the line of a scar from the side of his mouth to his eye; it gave him the appearance of a permanent, one-sided smile. He couldn't have been more than twenty-five, but he had the beer gut of a man twice his age. He watched as the woman in high heels swept past them and called out, in his gravely smoker's voice, "Those clothes make you look stupid!"

Michelle couldn't help it; she laughed. The guy sounded like a troll.

He took in her half-starved appearance and told her, in that same ridiculous voice, "Here, hold my puppy." The pit bull puppy, which he produced from inside his jacket, was shaking with cold and fear. His name was Milo. The guy who'd handed him to her was Scum.

After that, it was her job to take care of Milo when Scum got too drunk, which was every day if he could manage it. Like Michelle at the time, Scum considered himself basically asexual; he thought girls were stupid and gay guys were fags. Like her, he was also literate. A lot of those guys were; they'd get into these huge fights about who had bigger balls, Bukowski or Burroughs, and ten minutes later they'd be back to filling their empty forties with hocked-up wads of phlegm.

Scum's buddies had names like Cuddles and Jizm and Pussbucket, and they all had the kind of pants that would have stood up by themselves had they ever taken them off, stiffened by archeological layers of tar and food and patches they'd sewn by hand, of which they were deeply proud. They called her Skelly, because it rhymed with Shelly and because they said they could see her bones. Like her, they all had reasons for needing medication.

Just after Thanksgiving, it must have been, because they'd just returned from the Neon Jesus Mission, where the guys had stuffed themselves with turkey. Where even she, the queen of starvation, had put down an entire plate of mashed potatoes and green beans.

She and Scum were sharing a bottle under the bridge when a little truck with a camper top pulled over by the side of the parkway. Her first impression of Dyson had been of how small he was—a little man in a hat, a fedora, and a wool jacket over his hoodie. He could have been a college professor, she thought, watching him scramble up the embankment toward them. He could have been one of her teachers from high school. What the hell was he doing?

Milo, predictably, tried to jerk free from his leash and tear the guy's head off—Milo at that point no longer a shivering, freckled dog-baby but a full-grown, snarling pit bull with a mouth like a broken bottle.

Any normal person would have backed away. But any normal person would not have approached them under this bridge to begin with. Michelle caught her first glimpse of Dyson's eyes through those fogged glasses, that clear, steady blue. Scum whistled, finally, and Milo fell back on his haunches, flicking first one ear then the other.

"Are you hungry?" the little man asked them.

Jiz smiled like a wolf with missing teeth. "No," he said, "but we are thirsty. *Real* thirsty."

Cuddles cleared his throat and then cut one of those impossibly long and languid farts for which he was known. "You wouldn't happen to have any spare change now, would you, brother?"

"Or a sweater for our friend here?" Jiz indicated Pussbucket, who had passed out inside his old army jacket. "He's been feeling sort of sick."

Cuddles coughed, snorting back laughter. Michelle had not been wrong in her first impression of Scum, which applied equally to his friends: they lived under bridges, like trolls, and like trolls, they demanded payment from travelers. But they were essentially harmless, which the stranger seemed to know. He smiled.

"I've got some leftovers from Food Not Bombs," he told them. "Are you hungry?"

"Sure."

All eyes on her. Jiz had obviously been about to start working on the guy for his jacket. Now all he could do was stare as she, Skelly the skeleton, clambered down the embankment with the little man to his truck.

That blue Nissan with the cracked windshield, no bumper stickers. The camper shell looked even older than the truck, which looked older than she was. (Which, in fact, it was.)

The little man popped the tailgate, then the camper back, and turned to face her. "I'm Dyson."

"Shelly," she said. "Or Skelly. Whatever."

He hauled out an insulated beverage dispenser and a stack of reused yogurt containers and spoons. His truck, she saw, contained a bed, neatly made up with layers of blankets and quilts. All around it were books, lined up on homemade shelves rigged up with bungee cords. Most of the titles were unfamiliar, but there at the end of the shelf was her old friend Vonnegut, *Cat's Cradle*. She considered pocketing the book and also the candle beside it. Instead, she took a container of soup from Dyson as he handed it to her.

"I'm not sure I can eat all this," she said, peering into the container. She wasn't sure she could eat any of it, really, but the weather was cold and it felt good to have something warm in her hands. "Is it vegetarian?"

"Vegan." It must have been obvious from her expression that she'd never heard the word. "No dairy or animal products," he explained. "Here, have a seat." He indicated the tailgate next to him.

Her opportunity to gank his stuff now passed, she decided what the hell. She put a spoonful of soup in her mouth, pretty much for something to do. She didn't really have a plan. Maybe to take a few bites and leave it, just to see if she could piss him off.

"We were serving in the park when the rain came," he said. So softly it sounded like a secret.

"So you decided to just go find people to feed? Like, around the city?"

He nodded.

"Seems like a lot of work." She snuck a look up at the ledge under the bridge, where Jiz was urinating off the side. Scum raised an empty fifth in her direction in salute. Their fifth, which he'd emptied. "A lot of work for a pot of soup."

Dyson fixed her with a steady eye. "It's not just a pot of soup. It's embodied energy. Resources."

Michelle said nothing. Again, it must have been clear that she had no idea what he was talking about.

"It takes a lot of effort to turn a seed into a plant," he said, "and a plant into a vegetable. The way this food was raised, it probably took a lot of fertilizers and pesticides too, which take a lot of energy to produce. Then it took a lot of gasoline to get the food to the store, and after the store threw it out, it took me a lot of time to dig it out of the dumpsters, clean it and cook it and haul it out here."

"You jump in dumpsters?" Michelle had never seen anyone like him in a dumpster before.

Dyson just shrugged, like there were a lot of things about him that might surprise her. It was raining hard, the way it did sometimes in Portland when the clouds just sat down on the city, obliterating buildings, canceling the skyline and pounding the river opaque. Even under the shelter of the bridge, there was a cold mist, and her skin felt clammy. The container of soup wasn't warm anymore. She went to hand it back to him before she realized it was empty.

"You want more?" They were about eye level, still sitting on the tailgate. She pretended to consider his offer, considering instead the inside of his camper, his books and his bed.

"Do you need help?" she asked. "Like, serving food?"

She could hear the cars *shushing* through the rain on the bridge above them, the whine of a siren in the distance. Her own breath, catching on that last bit of a cold in her lungs that she hadn't been able to kick, living the way she did, outside, always exposed to the whims of the weather.

She wondered later, after he'd agreed, whether Dyson had heard it too—the slight wheeze in her lungs at the lower registers.

She spent the rest of the day driving around with him in the rain, finding people to feed—under bridges, under overpasses, and under gazebos in the park. A lot of those people seemed to recognize Dyson, and Michelle found that she liked how it felt to be with him, to be doing something useful for a change. Every time she dished up a bowl of soup for someone, she thought about what Dyson had said, about how much energy it took. The thought occurred to her on some level that if she could learn how to feed people, maybe she could learn how to eat.

At the end of the day, Dyson drove them to the Axxis Infoshop in Southeast. Food Not Bombs was based out of a little kitchen in the back there where they washed everything down in a couple of industrial sinks that had been salvaged from a canning factory on the coast.

The Axxis seemed like a cross between a house, a library, and a store. But a pay-what-you-can-maybe-barter-or-something type of store. She remembered being surprised that it was cold inside. Dyson explained that in order to save energy, the collective that ran the place had decided not to turn on the heat. "So," she said, "this is kind of a squat?"

He'd just nodded, the way he did when you asked a stupid question. Like it wasn't stupid at all. "Kind of," he said. "Except we pay rent."

Rent, he explained, was provided by donations from people attending classes at Axxis: workshops on do-it-yourself bicycle repair, natural childbirth, carpentry, you name it. Every inch of the place was handmade or recycled, and it functioned entirely on volunteer labor.

All of which maybe impressed her more as a scheme for freeloading than it did for its idealism. But that was understandable, considering who she was at the time, which really was not a whole lot more than your average little punk-ass hood. Left to her own devices, Michelle pocketed a book called the *Slingshot Organizer*, though she had no idea what that even was. Dyson walked out of the kitchen just as she was slipping it in her pocket.

"Put it back," he said.

"What?" she asked.

"That." He indicated the contents of her pocket.

Leaving her no choice but to place that little book back on its shelf. Clearly, her selfless feeding-the-hungry bit hadn't fooled him.

"Where do you want me to drop you off?" he asked.

She looked around at the collages on the floors of the Axxis—at the old Frigidaire in the back, stuffed full of dumpstered produce—at Dyson's truck through the window, parked in the driveway in the rain.

"What if I don't want you to drop me off?"

Was he thinking of her face, her body, the way she'd looked, dishing out soup in the park—that look they all had, sort of thin and cocky and scared? Or had he seen the scars on her arms, the mess she'd made of them the day before? All she'd been able to tell at the time was that he was working something out in his head.

"I want to stay with you," she said, "doing stuff like this." She lifted a hand, gesturing—at what, exactly? The little store, the kitchen through the open door, the yogurt containers they'd left to dry beside the sink?

Dyson lifted his chin. "On one condition."

He took a step closer, and she felt herself tense. Though what had she expected?

He opened his hand, palm up—he was holding an avocado. It was the first time she'd seen such a thing, as her folks weren't big on vegetables. She watched, amazed, as he peeled the dark skin off on one side, revealing that mysterious, pale-green interior.

The avocado was Dyson's only mandate: if she wanted to stay with him, she had to eat it.

The memory had faded a bit over the years, the way a photograph does when exposed too long to light. But when Michelle squeezed her eyes shut, alone at the table in the Black Cat, all of it came back—the silky, sensual texture of that avocado. The subtle taste of it. How at first she was not sure but then could not get enough.

Had Dyson shared such a moment with those other girls? Was it his standard M.O., perhaps, in nursing anorexics back to life? To go directly for the highest calorie content, the most fat? Was that avocado—her first taste of it, so achingly important in the story of her life—no more than a kind of pickup line for him, a ploy?

The sound seemed to come not through her voice box but through her head, so high-pitched it didn't even sound human. Before she could think about it, she'd stabbed the tip of her ballpoint pen into the open notebook. So hard it stayed there for a moment, stuck.

The world was watery, weepy, wandering every which way as she stood. And reached, the way she'd known she would, for the glass in the box on the shelf. Her lips clamped between her teeth, she worked the flaps open on top and then lifted it out of the box. *Hold onto your rage,* she told herself. *Use it like a weapon. Don't let it turn to despair.*

She took a breath. And then another, the way she'd trained herself to, even as she could feel some muscle deep down in her abdomen twitching. After a long moment, she let herself walk to the back door and then down the steps, out into the white-hot glare of the sun.

She stood in the driveway of the Black Cat, blinking back tears. Reminding herself that this was the world, the real world, with its trees and dirt and trash mixed in with cottonwood fluff and seed husks, all piled up together against the porch. What was in her head, these memories, were imaginary—real only insofar as they'd brought her here, to this. She'd been through the same thought process time and again when the things she remembered, running on a loop, threatened to suck her under: that moment in the drug counselor's office with her dad, the expression on his face as he'd struck her; the image of that forest across the highway from where she'd grown up, razed to dirt and twisted roots; those baby rabbits she'd found there, bulldozed and bloodied but not quite dead.

Michelle pulled a breath. And then another, focusing on small details: The blue tile in the mosaic paver. The coffee table made from a bent bike rim. The wrought-iron bike rack the barista at Rich's Roast had donated to the cause. The tip jar made out of an old milk jug they passed around at shows, which was sitting by the stage now, gathering grasshoppers. God help her, she loved this place. This shoddy, shabby house, with its yard full of sprung couches. She loved the way people had come together here to fight for what they loved.

That fight had mostly been met with defeat, the latest of which had come just that morning. But the Central Arizona Water Alliance had committed to appealing the judge's decision, all the way to the Supreme Court, if necessary. Was Michelle really just going to pack up this place and move on?

Everybody talked about the Black Cat being Dyson's legacy, but it was hers too—it was the legacy of anybody who claimed it as their own. Like the Navajo activists who'd used the Cat to disseminate their press releases. That scrappy coalition had won out in the end—the young native activists, full of fire, and the weary elders up on Black Mesa who'd been fighting their whole lives. After decades of occupation, they'd finally gotten that old coal company off the reservation. Off of Diné, the landscape of dreams, where she and Dyson had bowed their heads and made their vows, to the world and to each other.

A small victory, but against giants, what else was there?

Like her GED, her sobriety. Like staying alive this long. Like making the rent on this place each month.

Like everything else in her life.

Michelle could feel that hard knot starting to loosen inside her—and yet, it would not give. Because what about *Sylvie*, *Rachel*, and *Evangeline*? Had Dyson pledged his troth to them as well, in a time and place no one else would ever know or tell, in a ceremony no one had seen?

Were they as strong as she was? As resilient?

Or had they broken when he'd left them, those scared, cocky girls—those skinny, shivering runaways, like strays, who had no home in this world?

Michelle snapped that glass, as hard as she could, against the pavement.

And watched, incredulous, as it bounced.

The vessel had landed on the heaviest glass, at the base, and then just sort of jumped into the dirt beside the sidewalk. The damn thing hadn't even cracked. She could almost hear Dyson laughing.

And hell, maybe it was a joke.

Slowly, carefully, she picked up that miraculous glass and walked back inside to the kitchen. Where she poured herself some water and, taking her time, stood there at the sink, drinking it. Soon, she promised herself, she'd crack the fridge and find some food. The first few bites were always the hardest. But then the resistance would give way and her body would remember what it felt like to be part of this world.

Moving gently now, as if she might break all over again, Michelle returned to the table, lifted the old ballpoint pen from where it had fallen, and turned the pages of the notebook. Until the scar she'd made in the paper was no more than an impression, something you'd have to look closely to notice.

Dyson Lathe, she wrote, but then stopped.

What about Sylvie? she wanted to ask him. When you were twenty-eight and she was fifteen? What about Rachel, fourteen when you were thirty? What about me? Did we all just look like Evangeline, age thirteen, when you were a freshman in college?

She scratched out his name and then wrote it again. The way it was written inside her, she imagined, scratched out and rewritten, over and over again, in those hours she'd spent at this table, trying to find words for the sacred, the unspeakable, the deeply subterranean grieving in her that had nowhere to go.

Longtime activist Dyson Lathe, she wrote, *born Christopher Mason, has passed away at the age of forty-six, in an act of suicide sponsored by the state. He was a friend to many. He believed in the inherent worth of human beings and the natural world. He was a writer, an organizer, a humanitarian, and a pacifist. But when it came to the destruction of the things he held most dear, he did what any real revolutionary does. He walked into the fire. He laid his body on it.*

Again, the watery world went sideways. Because it was a lie, wasn't it? Dyson Lathe was a figment. Whoever he'd been under all those layers, all those half truths and omissions, all those fortune-cookie sayings, was someone almost wholly unknown to her.

The thought of this, like so many things, enraged her. But if she could still feel that pain, she figured, no vital nerves had been severed. She was alive—bruised, maybe, but unbroken.

Eight

Hot Season

Rell

TWO DAYS BEFORE THE FOURTH OF JULY, Rell awoke from siesta and stepped outside to check the temp, only to discover a pink-and-green hula-hoop hung on the hedge.

The thermometer on her neighbor's porch read 103 degrees.

This neighbor, as far as Rell knew, did not own a hula-hoop.

She walked back in the house and stuck her head in the freezer.

She'd been dreaming, she remembered, of water.

She'd been dreaming of the pink granite formations north of Crest Top that resembled softly pillowed mounds of mashed potatoes in places, and in others, the drip castles of little gods. In her dream, these rocks had been half-flooded, doubled, hung atop themselves in those tide pools endemic to the desert, full of cactus-like anemones and starfish saguaros. She'd spotted a ship in the distance, shimmering like a mirage.

When her head began to pound with cold, Rell shut the freezer door. And blinked, confronted with a card Jenna must have stuck there with that smiley-face magnet. *Tell me,* it said, *what is it you plan to do with your one wild and precious life?*

Rell let her eyes drift gently shut. *Fuck if I know.*

She'd spent the month since graduation in sort of a lucid daze, dozing through the day and napping at night, bullshitting in bars and lying out on the roof in the wee hours of the morn, gazing up at the stars. (This last was not so much romantic as pragmatic, as the house had no AC.) Katie had first moved out then dropped out; Jenna was still around, but she was spending most of her time these days with Crockett. Leaving Rell and the house to keep her own odd hours, which lent themselves to odd dreams.

She returned to the dim living room and paged through the chapter she'd been reading before falling asleep, from the book she'd all but stolen from the library, *Canada: C'est Magnifique!* She'd spent hours that summer turning its pages, with the Arizona sun blazing away behind those blinds, gazing in amazement at the ice castle built each year on the shores of Lake Louise, at sturdy huskies mushing between Aleut villages and ruddy-faced children in toques and toboggans. All that snow, pure porn amid such heat.

This book was part of a fantasy she'd developed about Canada. In this fantasy, come the fall, when the lease on the house was up, she'd drive north to B.C. and find herself a mountain town. She'd get a job slinging bagels—since her qualifications there, at least, were not in question—and come the spring, join one of the tree-planting crews that followed in the footsteps of the loggers.

Rumor had it you could make real money that way if you were tough enough to take it. Rell wasn't sure she was, but nearly any other option seemed worse. Say, for instance, selling her eggs. Which wasn't even really an option, because she smoked, though she could quit, and in fact she probably should—if nothing else, to cut expenses.

There were people who would have told Rell to take some time to figure out her next move, to cut herself some slack. But as far as she was concerned, those people were not all that good at math. Forty grand worth of debt divided by thirty rejected job applications times eight dollars an hour equaled a lifetime of lectures from her mother about how she should have just played it safe and gone to community college, which was not a fate Rell was prepared to endure.

What's more, she was sick of the news. There were no weapons of mass destruction at stake in Iraq, only another pipeline, one that ensured the U.S.'s unfettered access to oil. And maybe there were places in the U.S. where people had a problem with that, but Crest Top, as far as Rell could tell, was not one of them. The rodeo was set to kick off any day now, and every night for the last week, Ransom Row had been jammed with cowboys, both the real deal and the Scottsdale poseurs, the streets bumper to bumper with right-wing witticisms: *My God Is An Awesome God* (Oh yeah? Mine is better!); *Iraq: Let's Roll!* (Hey! Let's not!); *America: Love It Or Leave It!*.(I do, but thanks, maybe I will).

Cool, reasonable Canada, with its sustainable forestry practices; Canada, with its sensible gun laws and free, socialized health care; Canada, with its laughable mounties.

When the letter from Iowa arrived, it should have been the end of all that. This letter, which Rell almost felt as if she had dreamed, though there it sat on the kitschy wagon-wheel coffee table in the same spot it had occupied for the last two weeks. This letter contained an actual offer for an actual job, one she didn't even remember applying for, with the Iowa State Park Service. An entry-level office position, but it was secure and salaried and duly insured—hers, pending the background checks required by law, starting the first of August.

And yet, taking this job would mean moving to Decorah, Iowa, far from mountains of any type. It was a town where nothing much of any consequence had occurred, as far as Rell was aware of, since 500,000 years ago, when the glaciers had retreated, leaving behind some mildly acidic groundwater to cut the karst into caves. One of which possessed the paradoxical quality of forming stalactites of ice during the summer months.

Now, to make matters worse, Rell had gotten word that the Central Arizona Water Alliance was hiring an intern. With a tiny stipend provided entirely by a grant that would evaporate within a year. A stipend so small that in order for Rell to take the job, she would have to hold on to two shifts a week at Flip's just to stay off food stamps, never mind pay off her loans.

And yet, she couldn't help but think about it during her shifts at the bagel shop—couldn't help but turn it over in her head as she lay up there on the old-fashioned asphalt shingles of 737 Sycamore, counting the stars as they fell. Whenever Jenna showed up at the house, she seemed so rushed that Rell didn't feel like she could bring it up—and really, they'd never had that kind of relationship anyway. It was Katie Rell used to confide in. Katie, back before she'd become K, or whoever she was now, living at home with her parents.

In the absence of roommates, Rell felt herself unmoored, moving in slow motion that summer, adrift in a sort of limbo. If she was honest with herself, she'd been watching and waiting, searching for a sign.

Now here it was, nearly the Fourth of July—a week before the deadline to respond to that letter—and here she sat, still turning the pages of this book.

She read about the abundant rainfall in the Okanagan Valley, found herself dozing through an inset on the international jet set that swarmed Whistler in the winter—and started awake, once again, at that two-page spread on the winter festivities at Lake Louise.

That cold, fantastic castle seemed as improbable to her those stalactites of ice deep underground—as unlikely as that deluge in the Dells she'd dreamed.

Rell roused herself from the couch and drew the shades, threw open the windows, and turned loose the front door. Outside, the pale-blue sky had darkened to dusk, and the rodeo had begun. She could hear the national anthem in the distance, followed by a roar of applause.

The Arizona Territory Round Up and Rodeo sounded like the Super Bowl, sounded like the crowds at the Coliseum. When Rell squeezed her eyes shut, she could see the sea of oversized RVs out there at the rodeo grounds, all those F450s and behemoth SUVs. All these red-blooded Americans, packing heat.

It was, by all accounts, the hottest summer on record in Crest Top. Each day the clouds gathered at noon, but rain refused to fall. Whole hillsides of ponderosa pines had dried and died, their needles gone brittle and blond. The air so still the wind from a wasp's wings could have blown the forest alight.

And still those pretend soldiers soldiered on, burning up the carbon deposited by the swamps of the Paleozoic, a gallon of the stuff every five miles or so. Bought and paid for, she could not help but think, with blood—that of real people, real soldiers. Not to mention some seriously fucked up rewiring of the human heart.

Yet there sat Cougar Butte at the end of the street, shimmering and serene, with the sun sinking toward it like a Valkyrie funeral pyre. Beyond the apartment building across the street, she could just make out the shoulder of Quartz Mountain, a gentle swell to the north. To the east, where the sky had gone that glassy, cobalt blue, lay the grasslands of Wind Valley, and to the south, Bridal Creek. The whole of the landscape stretched out inside her, the map she'd made of memories in the course of backcountry classes and field trips, mountain bike rides, and long solo hikes—from which she'd returned, each time, with the sense of having been initiated into mysteries.

When Rell thought of leaving this place, something in her gut clenched, as if steeling itself for the blow.

The crowd in the distance exploded into applause—like a crop of fireworks, bursting and subsiding. And she might have been half-asleep still and half-dreaming, but it sounded like the war itself they were cheering on.

Her gaze drifted back to the driveway. That pink-and-green hula-hoop, she saw, was still hung on the hedge.

Which was looking increasingly crisp.

* * *

Walking toward the bike trail that night, Rell caught wind of a song. It was a wordless sort of personal blues, and it quieted as she grew closer. A slight figure stood atop the massive cottonwood that had fallen that winter, its huge heart hollowed out.

"What up, Arin."

"What up, Rell."

In the moonlight Arin's brown skin glowed blue. "That there hoop looks dangerous," she said.

Rell looked down at the hula-hoop on her shoulder. "It might be," she allowed.

"You got a permit for that thing?"

"Naw. You think they'll let me take it into the bar?"

Arin appeared to consider that. "Depends on which bar."

Her boots hit the dirt with a thud as she dropped from her perch on the fallen tree. Arin wore those old Docs year round, despite the heat, and they lent her a kind of gravity, like that strangely serious façade. But all this, Rell had come to see, was simply to keep her from floating away; Arin moved like a bit of cottonwood fluff picked up by the wind.

"What do you got going this evening?" Arin asked her.

Rell stubbed the toe of her Chaco into the dirt. "You know Natalie? The bartender at Billy Jack's?"

"Red hair? Tattoos?" Rell nodded, and Arin said, "I went to school with her brother."

Natalie was a fire dancer, a burlesque performer, a sort of circus unto herself. The lady knew all the tricks with bottles and pours behind the bar, and sometimes at the end of her shift she'd step outside into the street with her chains and throw down, in that sassy red corset she wore sometimes to work. Rell had thought maybe she'd just bring this here hula-hoop on down to Billy Jack's and see what Natalie could do—a little Burning Man for the rodeo crowd.

But now, standing here with Arin, Rell felt embarrassed to admit this. As if in bringing up Natalie—who was probably as much responsible for Rell's nightly patronage as Billy Jack's two-for-one Sierra Nevadas—she'd confessed to something.

"I don't know," she said. "I had some sort of mission in mind. Something to do with Natalie. And this hoop."

"Seems reasonable."

"Does it?"

Arin shrugged. Like, at this time of year, pretty much anything could be considered reasonable.

Rell cleared her throat. "I actually just woke up." Though in a way, that was confessing something too. "How about you? What are you doing tonight?"

"Me?" Arin whistled—not like a person but like a bird. "I'm headed out to the ocean."

Rell grinned. "The ocean, eh?" She was practicing her Canadian.

"The ocean. Yes." Like there was nothing the least bit odd about that, these four hundred miles from the closest coast, these five thousand feet above the sea.

"I was just dreaming about the ocean," Rell told her. "About a tide pool filled with barrel cactus, blooming. Out in the Dutchman's Dells."

"Sounds like a sign."

Rell studied her face. Because hadn't she, Rell, gone so far as to admit it? That she was, at that point, looking for something wholly irrational—some omen to make itself known to her? "A sign of what, do you think?"

Arin just cocked her head. As if Rell were a slow child, or a smart dog. "I don't know," she said. "You tell me."

A night bird somewhere sang. "The ocean," Rell said.

"The ocean."

"That's where you're headed tonight."

"It is indeed."

"Is it close?"

"You know," Arin told her, "it's closer than you'd think."

Was this a form of flirtation? Or no more than a bit of whimsy, a loosening of that impassive mask Arin seemed to wear by day? Rell considered her, and Arin considered her in return. Her eyes were dark, depthless pools, her thick eyebrows incongruous on her delicate face. Really, those eyebrows were Rell's favorite feature of hers; they made her look like someone you could tell your secrets to.

"You should come with me," Arin said. "To the ocean."

Rell did not know what this invitation was an invitation to. But it occurred to her that for once, she did not need to know. She had no real plans but to turn this morning's tips into that night's beer. The night was young, wasn't it?

And still, most likely, over ninety degrees.

In one fine, fluid motion—as if it were a sport she'd been training for in her dreams—Rell lifted the hoop from her shoulder and tossed it high in the air. It landed on the sign at the end of Second Street, encircling those two stern words: *DEAD END.*

* * *

They walked in silence along the trail beside the creek, through the cool shadows of the cottonwoods. They transpired moisture, those trees, from deep underground, their breath the ghost of water in the night. This was one of the things Rell had found she liked about Crest Top in the summer, the way hidden things were revealed.

Like the town's slacker intellectuals and deadbeat dreamers, its hotshot firefighters and geologists and backcountry guides, who seemed to come out of the woodwork at night; she felt embarrassed now to have called them townies. And all those cool green swimming holes of upper Bridal Creek—how had she managed to miss them? Maybe she'd just been moving too fast. There was something about the pace of summer here, the stillness of it. She liked the way the clouds had begun to roll in each afternoon, dark with the promise of rain—the dreamy way the cottonwood fluff let loose from the trees and piled up amongst the weeds in fuzzy white drifts, like snow.

That snow of seeds lay at the feet of the saplings that Rell had helped to plant—in the moonlight, their white plastic socks seemed to glow. Part of her wanted to be here to see those trees grow tall, wanted to see this part of the greenway become indistinguishable from the rest. As they rounded Quartz Creek Park, Rell wondered, were there cottonwood trees in Iowa? Big, greedy trees that sucked up water from forty feet around and spread out in great arches overhead? Trees that burned the brightest canary yellow, come autumn, against the blinding blue of the sky? As they passed the band shelter, Rell could not help but remember that picture of Katie from the Cat, at that first protest she'd attended, with the yellow leaves of the cottonwood trees strewn like embers at her feet.

Katie, who'd nearly set the better half of the state on fire, trying to save the Greene—as if any sort of grand gesture like that would ever change anything. Rell shook her head as she walked. Real change was nothing but long, slow, pissy work, of the sort she'd grown sick of here in Crest Top, fighting the pipeline.

Maybe that was why she hadn't been able to let go of the fantasy of Canada, though it made no sense at all. Because it seemed as if it would be simple, the way nothing else seemed simple, to rise each day, aching and sore, to plant trees—to walk among the fallen boreal forests, both clear cut and partial, and do absolutely nothing but sink the small, hopeful plug of a tree in the ground, to shore up its supports and move on. Speed, they said, was the key to making money planting trees, and that was what Rell wanted—to align what she had to do for money with what she wanted to do for the world, and to work, like a piston, like an oil rig, bending her back to some great cause. To do what she could and move on.

But if the dream she'd had that day, asleep in the heat, was indeed a sign, what kind of a sign was it? So detailed in its depictions of topography, its fractal geometry—such a dream could leave no doubt as to the accuracy of the map inside her. And yet the Dutchman's Dells had been flooded, the way northeast Iowa had been at the end of the last ice age. And that ship—didn't it suggest some significant departure, a journey to distant lands?

It occurred to Rell as they crossed the bridge over Quartz Creek, in the dry sauna of the deepening night, that this is what the desert did to you eventually. Something about the colors, the quality of light, the way great stretches of time seemed written in the rocks, both in their shapes and negative spaces. Something about the way the desert cooked your brain, even as it granted access to vast vistas; the line between dreams and waking blurred.

Like the tumbled white stones of Quartz Creek, entirely exposed now, entirely dry. Though they were no more than chunks of silicon dioxide washed down from the Bradshaws during the course of great floods, long before the founding of Crest Top, in the moonlight they seemed imbued with significance. No wonder all those New Agers had convinced themselves of the curative properties of quartz; it looked like chunks of the moon itself had fallen to earth here. Before Rell knew it, she'd be deciphering the hieroglyphics of prehistoric sea slug trails and spotting lights moving at right angles in the sky.

"Something on your mind?" Arin asked as they passed beneath the railroad trestle.

"The alliance is hiring an intern."

"I heard. You going to apply?"

"I don't know. The pay is peanuts." Even as Rell said the word, ridiculously, she felt her stomach rumble. She hadn't really eaten dinner, another consequence of the heat. She stopped by the horseshoe pits at the end of the bike trail and picked up a ring. "You play?"

Arin picked up a horseshoe lying in a pile of cottonwood fluff and blew it off. "You first."

Rell sighted the rebar, but then she tossed the horseshoe the way she had the hoop, without giving it much thought. It rung the stake like a bell.

Arin stepped up to the line. She hefted her horseshoe aloft, and it sailed through the air. Once again, that bell rang out in the night.

They turned to one another and grinned. Clearly, they were in the zone.

And yet, Rell felt her stomach cramp, insistently this time. "You aren't hungry, are you?"

"You want me to make you a sandwich?"

Rell laughed. As if Arin had just suggested that sandwich ingredients grew wild here in the woods along Quartz Creek—that a sandwich might just drop down on them from the branches above.

"No, seriously. We're three blocks from the bakery. I've got my keys." Arin held them up and shook them in the shadows. The keys glittered mysteriously.

Downtown, pimped-out pickups were booming Top 40 country, and Ransom Row was a sea of Stetsons, not to mention weekend warriors in Harley-Davidson gear and a douchey assortment of Phoenix frat boys. As they crossed Hall Street, a pickup truck plastered with American flags nearly ran them over. The driver lay down on his horn as he passed.

Arin shook her head. "Fucking rednecks."

Slipping into the alley behind Ransom Row that night felt like stepping behind the set in a Western. This row of brick shops had been rebuilt in the late eighteen hundreds, when the entire block caught on fire; not much had changed about it since then, and if the historic society had anything to do with it, not much ever would. Quietly, they scaled the steps to the back door of the bakery. Arin turned her magic key in the lock, and together, they slipped inside.

The lights were on in front to discourage burglars, but the kitchen was dim, lit only by the blue face of the microwave display and the green digital clock on the wall. It looked like the lights in an aquarium, or a pool after hours. Arin cracked the fridge, and Rell hopped up on a stool by the pastry bench. "How about that brown-sugar-brie-and-apple thing you guys do?"

"You want fries with that?"

Rell watched the way Arin gathered her ingredients—presliced Granny Smiths and slabs of sticky cheese, separated by wax paper—the way she spun the loaf of sourdough free from its plastic bag. The way she buttered the bread and sprinkled the sugar, piled apples and cheese and flicked on the Panini press, all without turning on the lights. The whole operation was over in a matter of minutes. "Damn," Rell said, as Arin lay her sandwich, steaming, on a plate before her.

"You need light?" Arin stood by the switch by the door.

"No." Rell said it quickly, feeling protective of this moment, the half light they inhabited, here among the bulk bins of organic flour and the meat slicer, its stainless steel gleaming faintly in the streetlight from the window. It was that summertime thing—the way daylight felt too bright, overexposed. The dark was restful, peaceful, full.

"Suit yourself," Arin said.

"Here, share this with me."

"I don't eat cheese."

"Just have the apples."

So she did. There in the bakery at night, in the dark, with the patriotic party outside, it felt like they were sharing a secret.

Rell turned to Arin. "Question."

"All right."

"Have you ever turned down a job offer?"

Arin picked apple skin out from between her teeth. "This is pretty much the only job I've ever had. Unless you count community service."

Rell nodded, though she wasn't sure what she was agreeing with.

"Just stupid shit. Junior high."

Rell crunched into a pocket of brown sugar and chewed it slowly, letting the crystals dissolve to syrup on her tongue. "I got this offer. From a state park in Iowa. They want me to start in September."

"Congratulations."

Rell nodded again, as if congratulating herself, though it felt more like an attempt at consolation. "It's in my field, at least—native plant conservation."

"You should be psyched."

"I should."

"Is it out in the middle of a cornfield? Big Corn State Park?"

"No. It's by a river. There's this cool cave system nearby."

"Coldwater Cave?"

"You know the place?"

"Biggest cave system in the Midwest, right? Something like twenty miles long. All kinds of fossilized sea lilies down there, five hundred million years old."

"No shit." Rell studied Arin's face, though the half light here wasn't the issue; it was that mask she wore, that neutral reserve that revealed nearly nothing. "How do you know all that?"

"My high school biology teacher, Mr. Rosenwald."

There they sat in the kitchen of the bakery, the only place Arin had ever worked. As Rell set that empty plate down on the pastry bench before her, she tried to think of a way to ask: Was Arin planning on going to college? Rell had never heard anything from her to that effect—no plans for the future at all, so far as she could recall. Was Arin too cool for school? Or just sort of stuck in the dream of this place, lost in limbo?

It came back to Rell, the way she'd come upon Arin that evening, standing in the shadows atop that fallen cottonwood, singing to herself, as if waiting for something—perhaps that ship Rell had dreamed to drift down Quartz Creek in the froth of some great flood, to anchor itself just long enough, there in the heart of this high-desert town, to carry her off to sea.

Arin stood. "The ocean."

"Yes."

"You good?"

As they pushed out the front door of the bakery onto Ransom Row, they found themselves engulfed in sound. The Friday night dance was underway at the Silver Spur, and that Tim McGraw song that was tearing up the airwaves these days spilled out through its swinging doors and onto the street, where the line to get in now stretched clear around the block. Rell took a step closer to Arin to keep from having to shout as they walked down the sidewalk, and two young women in high-waisted Wranglers stared uncharitably at them as they passed. Unimpressed, it seemed, by Arin's shaved head and Rell's unshaved shins.

"I believe these ladies think we're thespians," Rell said, loud enough for them to hear.

"Well, then, we ought to put on a show." Arin took Rell's hand, and they smiled sweetly at one another as they turned and jaywalked Geronimo.

The Crest Top County Courthouse was covered in patriotic bunting like a turn-of-the-century presidential campaign train car. In the plaza, four American flags lit up with floods festooned each side of the gingerbread gazebo; the bronze soldier at the Vietnam memorial was holding a tiny American flag in one hand, as if waving to a parade, and little American flags were pinned like gas-line notices amongst the red, white, and blue petunias at his feet.

Rell was reminded of the discovery she'd made as a child that any word could be divested of meaning through repetition: the, the, the, the, the, the, the, the, the, the, the, the, the, the, the, the, the, the, the, the, the, the, the, the, the, the, the, the, the, the, the, the, the, the, the, the, the, the, the, the, the, the, the, the, the, the, the, the, the, the, the, the, the, the, the, the, the, the, the, the, the, the, the, the, the, the, the, the, the...it occurred to her, crossing the courthouse plaza with Arin, that all those flags, for her, since 9/11, had been reduced to a long string of *the*s.

And yet, not two weeks previous, the U.S. death toll in Iraq had topped that of the population of Trafford, Pennsylvania, Rell's hometown. She wondered, what would the soldier at the Vietnam memorial—his arm uplifted, mouth open—have to say about this war? If he could speak, what would he say?

When they'd reached the hill at the top of Crook Street, she turned to Arin and said, "You ever think about Canada?"

Arin smiled gently at her. As if Canada were a great and beautiful snow-covered hope they both held dear.

They were standing beside the storefront of Hometown Heating and Cooling, which advertised free AC inspection. A piece of gum had adhered to Rell's sole; she worked it off, scudding her sandals on the hot concrete. "I hear Vancouver's pretty cool. And hey, it's right on the ocean!"

"Not this ocean," Arin said.

"What about Montreal?"

Arin looked up and searched the sky. "This ocean was before Montreal. Before all wars and holidays. Before all human habitation."

"Are you telling me that we're walking all the way to this prehistoric ocean? Won't that take, possibly, millions of years?"

Arin was moving again now, and Rell had to hustle to keep up. Arin said, "Not if we hop the train."

"I didn't know Crest Top had a train."

"Right here on McConnell Street was where the Chinese railroad workers used to live."

Rell blinked and adjusted a contact that had gone dry. "Did you actually grow up here?"

"Pretty much. Here, let's take a shortcut."

Rell followed her down a delivery alley full of broken-down boxes and restaurant traps reeking of grease to the grocery store parking lot; they crossed the hot asphalt with the sodium lights buzzing above. All around them, scowling retirees in sweat suits and golf shirts were toting carts full of Ho-Ho's and ground beef. For the first time that night, Rell began to wonder what it was she was doing.

"This doesn't look like the ocean to me."

Arin laughed, a nearly soundless sound. "This isn't the ocean." They were standing on a patch of dry grass beside the pseudohistoric building that housed a strip mall, across the parking lot from the grocery store at the intersection of Powell and Geronimo, which stood across the street from the bike trail. Arin climbed a set of concrete steps to a picnic table and said, "This is the train station."

Beside them was the sandwich shop, the frozen yogurt joint, and the local office of a national insurance franchise. Arin gazed serenely at each in turn, as if duly pleased with these exemplars of modern commerce. It was a look that struck Rell as less playful than possibly crazy.

Slowly, she rotated in place.

The storefronts, the parking lot, and the traffic remained unchanged.

The light at the intersection of Quartz Creek Road and Powell flashed from red to green.

The sign beside her read *The Depot Marketplace.*

Then her vision shifted and she saw it, like the second image in an optical illusion: The old train station had been turned into the strip mall; the pseudohistoric building was an actual historic building. The old train tracks had been turned into the bike trail; she'd passed beneath that old railroad trestle every day on her way to work—had passed beneath it that very night as they emerged from the bike trail—and yet it had never really occurred to her that, once upon a time, a train had run upon it.

Again, Arin whistled. It was a specific birdcall, Rell knew, but she didn't know what the bird was called.

"That old Santa Fe," Arin said. "It's running about a hundred years behind." She took five or so steps to her right, to the little blue pickup truck parked in the lot beside them. She popped the handle and hopped up into the driver's seat.

But now Rell had begun to wake from this half-awake state she'd been carried along by since she'd awoken from siesta. She hesitated for a moment, considering the truck—a relic of the eighties, it looked dented but indestructible, with three shades of paint showing through a long scratch on the passenger-side door. She approached it, and after a period of ineffectual yanking, it creaked open. She leaned in. "How far is it, would you say, to the ocean?"

Arin leaned in across the gearshift. "Honey," she said, "this is the only train for the next hundred years. If you want to go, you better get in."

* * *

Driving west up Cougar Butte Road, bits and pieces of Rell's dream came back to her. The memory of this dream inside her was like an immense piece of classical music, or a play with large set pieces and props. She told Arin, "I was dreaming of the desert, but the desert was also the ocean. Sometimes the water would evaporate, like a mirage. Other times, this ship would appear. It had sails someone had sewn together from old bed sheets and T-shirts, and they streamed out on either side of it like wings."

Arin said nothing, shifting gears around the long curves at the base of Cougar Butte.

"There were all these very precise transcriptions of form and structure. The barrel cactus were also sea urchins, and the ocotillo, octopi. A flock of finches turned and banked and shifted in flight, just like a school of fish."

The hum of the motor and the warm air through the open windows conspired in a kind of reverie. After a period of time, Arin spoke. "When I was a kid, I wanted to be a marine biologist. My grandmother is from Mexico, and she used to watch a lot of American TV when I was little, trying to learn English. It must have been something I saw on PBS."

"You ever been to Mexico?"

Arin shook her head no, easing the brakes around a turn.

"I actually had a class last fall in Mexico. In marine biology." Seized by synchronicity, Rell went on to describe Deep Canyon College's conservation center on the Sea of Cortez, its partnership with Arizona State. She went on like that for quite some time, stealing glances at Arin on the side; she nodded at the sea turtle hatchery, the whale watch, and the mangrove plantings, like she'd heard all about this place. But when Rell stopped, she was silent, like her mind had been somewhere else the whole time.

"I'll have to check that out," Arin said, finally, and finally, Rell understood that studying marine biology in Mexico, to Arin, seemed about as feasible as shooting golf on the moon.

Then they were hitting the switchbacks at a speed that seemed suddenly excessive, and a moment later they were flying around the turns, cutting corners and tooling around divots, dust rising up through the windows. Rell gripped the Jesus handle; to one side of the road, she knew, was an arroyo studded with boulders, and to the other, the sheer drop to Dead Horse Valley.

"Don't worry," Arin told her. "I learned to drive out here."

They hit a bump, and the pendant on the necklace that hung from the rearview mirror hit the windshield. Rell caught it. "What's this?"

"An extinct nautilus. Came with the truck."

The truck, Rell remembered, had been a gift from the late Dyson Lathe. "That's crazy, dude just gave you his ride."

Arin shrugged, like it wasn't so crazy, all things considered.

"What did you mean, what you said to Katie that day? About there being things about him you'd rather not know?"

Arin was silent for a long time, and Rell wondered if maybe she'd overstepped the bounds of this thing between them, this increasing sense of intimacy they'd established in the shadows of the bike trail, in the underwater light of the bakery kitchen. But then Arin spoke. "Dyson had a thing for young girls. Probably you could tell, right? His girlfriend, Michelle—she's your age. They got together when she was sixteen."

Rell nodded, like she'd known that, though she couldn't quite say she had.

"But." Arin stopped. "I don't know how to say it. It's just—he wasn't creepy about it. He just liked young people, fucked-up ones especially. It was like he took in stray dogs. And there's an age, as a young girl, where maybe you're interested to see what kind of effect you can have. It's not like you have any idea what you're doing. When young girls acted like that toward him, basically, he didn't discourage it. That's how you could tell there was something wrong with him. But it's not like I ever felt unsafe around him."

Rell tried not to show her discomfort. She didn't want to discourage the openness Arin had shown in speaking to what was obviously a fraught subject.

"My mom lives in this sort of group home situation in Tucson. Dyson knew I had no way to go see her, so he let me borrow his truck whenever I needed to. When he figured the feds were headed his way, he gave it to me. He thought the truck would be a liability. Some kind of history with it."

"Like what? It was stolen?"

"Something like that."

Again, Rell caught the pendant as it swung. The nautilus was a tiny version of the ones she'd seen in photographs, embedded in porous limestone. "How did he know they were coming for him? Do you know?"

"You ever meet his friend Huckleberry?"

"I've heard of him."

"Huck was the youngest of the crew that blew the Snoquomish Dam. He'd gotten word one of their old friends was working with the feds, part of plea-bargain deal. Dyson went north, Huck went south. Hitchhiking, or busing it, who knows." Arin nodded as she spoke, or maybe it was just a kind of rhythm in her body as she drove. "We figured all this out later. Me and Michelle."

Rell sat back in her seat, looking down at the dirt that had collected on the floorboards beneath her feet. Dirt from who knows where. "They caught Dyson. What about Huck?"

"No one knows."

Rell looked out into the dark and saw Katie there, the image of her up on the basalt ridge at the Bonner Ranch, her hair both green and blond, shaved on one side, in her desert camo—the revolutionary she'd wanted to be. How close she had come to a fate like Dyson's, like Huck's.

The fossilized nautilus swung back and forth, keeping time as the truck climbed. Rell watched Arin's hands as she drove. Delicate, their structure, like the bones of a bird—had those hands touched Dyson, the old man who liked young girls? *It's not like I ever felt unsafe around him.* From what Arin had said, Rell really couldn't tell. But she could not help but feel curious about those hands, just that night having held one of them in her own.

The dirt road wound its way up Cougar Butte, until finally it turned out into the parking lot presided over by the Forest Service sign announcing that they had reached the Cougar Butte trailhead. Arin pulled the truck into park, and they stepped out into the night. The air was as warm as bathwater.

"Which way?" Rell asked. Though by then she knew.

"Up."

"In the dark?"

Arin raised a hand. The moon was full overhead.

"What about the snakes?"

"The snakes are sleeping."

Arin was right; the trail through the forest was clear—clearer than it appeared by day, when the glare of the sun flattened all those fine details. In the blue moonlight, the berries of the manzanita hung in delicate clusters beside the trail, the bark of the ponderosas formed an intricate jigsaw puzzle, and the broad pads of the prickly pear glowed a cool, Martian green.

Somewhere out there, Rell knew, coyotes were stalking jackrabbits the size of small kangaroos and mule deer were stepping gingerly through the forest. She could see it all in her mind's eye, could sense the minutest of movements in the fine, dry molecules of the air; a sense of hyper-real perception enveloped her body like a membrane.

Over the years, Rell had hiked this trail in heat and snow, in monsoon rains and even once during a freak hailstorm in May. Every bend in the trail and every boulder here was known to her, in a way even the eastern woodlands of her childhood were not. This was the place where she had come to know herself in relation to the landscape, to read the altitude in the tree line, the rainfall in the sap.

They fell into step together, breathing in time through the switchbacks, slowing over the steeper stretches and quickening where the grade gave way. The ponderosas disappeared as they gained altitude, and at last they reached the rock face at the end of the trail. Avoiding a patch of hedgehog cactus that appeared to have been poured between two boulders, they scaled the flat rock near the top of Cougar Butte to Cougar's Perch.

The moon hung high in the sky, and all of Crest Top and Wind Valley lay stretched out before them, bathed in its underwater glow. The lights of town twinkled, bounded by long sweeps of rangeland.

"Ah," Rell said. "The ocean."

Arin settled weightlessly beside her. "All of this was underwater eighty million years ago."

Rell blinked at the image that rose up before her: waves lapping at their feet.

"The Western Interior Sea, they called it. Full of plesiosaurs and bad-ass prehistoric sharks. They've found these giant fossilized clams all over the Great Plains, all the way down to New Mexico." Arin's gaze encompassed the horizon. "Mr. Rosenwald used to bring us out here."

"Mr. Rosenwald would be proud." Rell could have stopped there, but she was feeling bold. The way maybe cougars had once felt, looking down on the lights of town. "You should check out that place I was telling you about in Mexico."

Arin cast her a glance.

"For real."

Arin lay back on the rock, her smile like a cactus flower, like a sea anemone, opening. "I've always wanted to go to Mexico. Or Costa Rica. Get outside the U.S. and take a look around, you know? See what's up."

Rell studied Arin's face. They'd known each other for years, but outside the pipeline protests and work, she'd only ever seen Arin a handful of times, as far as she could recall—once at the coffee shop, once at the Black Cat, and once with an old Hispanic woman in the barrio. They'd been pruning roses together, Arin and that old lady, their movements so deeply habituated to one another, so intimate, that Rell had felt embarrassed of herself, the way she was staring, and had turned away before catching Arin's eye. It occurred to Rell—strangely, for the first time—that old woman was Arin's grandmother. Arin lived there in the barrio with her. Which made them practically neighbors. And yet, Rell knew almost nothing about her life.

How was it, then, that she sensed in Arin the kind of connection she'd been looking for in college and ultimately failed to find? The kind of connection that might stand the test of time. She could see them traveling together, sharing in these sorts of epic adventures, following the signs. Maybe they'd explore the cenotes of the Yucatan, the coastal ecology of Costa Rica. Maybe they'd see that cold ice castle built each year on the shores of Lake Louise.

Maybe they'd just slip out of this whole mess that was the U.S. and take a look around.

And yet, she wondered, if they left, who would be here to sit out on Cougar's Perch come the full moon in July? Who would be here to fight for the Greene? For the Yaqui catfish and the leopard frog—for every little living thing that all the big things depended on?

If they left the country, who'd be left to say what the country was?

Rell reached out and took Arin's hand. The way, earlier that evening, Arin had taken hers. This time, though, for whatever reason, whatever they'd been pretending before was real. They were sitting close now, their bodies a single shadow on the rocks, limned in moonlight.

With Arin's small bird's hand warm in her own, Rell looked out over the lights of town, over the desert that had once been an ocean, and thought, *Who's to say what's possible?*

* * *

They'd pulled up down the street from the Black Cat, where Arin generally left the truck, to find an elaborate double-decker tour bus parked beneath a streetlight. The thing was covered in murals and mosaics and reflective spangles like some kind of elaborate Pakistani lorry. It looked as if someone had welded a VW bus on top of a Bluebird— it was cranking out a stream of bubbles from the emergency hatch of its back door. As they drew closer, they could see that the Jolly Roger hung limp on top.

"Holy shit," Rell said, "it's the ship."

"The ship?"

"From my dream."

Sure enough, someone had even hung their bedding from the windows to dry. The bus bore Colorado plates and smelled of french fries; its mirrored mosaics reflected them in pieces as they circled it. And now they could hear the show in progress at the Cat, a sideshow barker's call.

"*Step right up and step right in! Accept no substitutes!* Dr. Davis's Magic Sand is the most famous in all the land! My sand cures all dispositions, preexisting conditions, post-traumatic stress disorder, crises of conscience, depression, repression, and fear of surveillance! My competitor will try to mislead you with false claims regarding *his* Magic Sand, but his magic sand is a sham!"

And then a second voice, lower: "Ladies and gentlemen, boys and girls, let it be known that *my* sand is the finest in all the land. Dr. *Dayton*'s Magic Sand is the cure for high blood pressure, moral turpitude, loss of moral rectitude, male erectile dysfunction, jock itch, athlete's foot, anthrax, and terrorist attacks! This is the true, original, unblemished sand, made right here in the U.S. of A!"

As they approached the Cat, Rell could see that virtually everyone under the age of thirty still kicking around town that summer was sitting on a blanket or those old couches, leaning together in the doorway or balanced on the railing; a few had even found seats on the sagging roof. Rell knew them all, one way or another, from the bagel shop, the coffee shop, and the bars. These people were her people, her compatriots, her tribe.

She and Arin took their place among them, and now they could see that a spotlight shone on two performers standing beside the fence. Each stood atop a box labeled *SOAP BOX*, and each had a trunk set up so as to display a clutch of calcified medicine bottles labeled in swirling script. One performer had spiked hair and facial piercings and a long, toothy grin; the other was short and swarthy and looked like he'd slept in his whiteface.

"*Blasphemy!*" cried Spike. "Behold! The sand of our forefathers! The pure, unblemished sand!"

In his patchy face-paint, Shorty was livid. "Silence! Partake only of the sand of liberty! Of justice! The One True Sand!"

"Your sand has no constitutional basis! Your sand is a sham!"

"Your sand has no backbone! Your sand will wither from this land!"

"Believe not in the false sand!"

Someone let loose a hoot, and a guitar player lit into a swing. A woman had appeared stage left clad in nothing but a black bra and a pair of lacy, ruffled underwear. As they watched, she stepped out onto the stage, swaying sinuously, and behold, it was the One True Natalie, Rell's bartender from Billy Jack's—swinging, seriously *swinging* that pink plastic hula-hoop with the swirling green stripe.

She swung that hoop like it was a dust devil, a lasso—swung it like a cool breeze on a hot summer's night. She swung that damn hoop like it was the only thing in the world worth doing, down one arm, over her head, and, while the rowdy crowd whistled and moaned, down around her ruffles.

Shorty produced two chains of poi and lit them off. Without missing a beat, Natalie took the chains, one in each hand, and spun fire overhead as she swung.

The hoop is the symbol of all things fixed and evolving, she would tell them later in the bus. *The hoop is the axis, that motion that must be maintained.* She said the hoop was a tribute to the electrons that held them in place by spinning, to dust and stars and planets in orbit, satellites blinking in the ocean of space.

She told them, more specifically, that she'd been walking home from her shift at the bar that night and found the hoop encircling the sign beside the bike trail. A moment later, she'd spied the ship, and then the show.

She was beautiful, Natalie, maybe dangerously so. Because she wasn't afraid, even as the flames grazed her skin.

One by one, people stood, their lighters flickering in the air. Wordlessly, Rell and Arin rose to join them, and Rell lifted her Bic overhead. Hot, that little flame, hovering above her thumb. Risky, given the current climate.

But this was still the West, wasn't it? And still, the West was wild.

In the heat of the night, Rell found herself warming to that fire, as if she'd been born to it. *Shake it up, girl,* she thought. *Shine.*

Epilogue

Dead Man's Revival

THE SHOW THAT NIGHT had boiled down to a party, and the party had boiled down to this: nine people propped up on pillows and each other, listening to Jenna picking clawhammer banjo with the Devil. They sang cottonpicking tunes and hobo blues, and later, when an accordion appeared, a long series of sea shanties. Those nine being Rell and Arin; Jenna and Crockett; Dyson's girlfriend, Michelle; Natalie; and the members of the show on tour: the Geek (or the Greek), the Freak, and the Devil. They were known as the Dead Man's Revival.

While the music unwound, they all swilled off a jug of the hellacious corn liquor someone had managed to coax from a makeshift still that summer. The taste was explosive but the effect was correct: there arose between them an invisible campfire, burning their cheeks with goodwill.

The Devil laid off the accordion. It wheezed, drooping, as he lifted a limpid hand. "Ladies and gentlemen," he said, "hear ye now this sorrowful tale. Of larcenous lechery, patriotic acrimony, and the best of intentions gone awry."

"Not to mention," said the Freak, "some very ill shit."

Jenna giggled and then hiccuped, which made everyone laugh. She caught Rell's eye and winked; Rell and Arin were sitting together in a bean bag chair. No longer holding hands, but shoulder to shoulder, their arms across their knees.

"In the Year of Our Lord 1990 or so," the Devil said, "my esteemed colleague the Freak and I were traveling through a land inhabited by a hostile race known as Hoosiers. We passed a night at a Love's Truck Stop, and there we were propositioned by a large man with a mullet, a member of the local militia."

"Tyson," said the Freak. "Like the chicken."

"When we failed to perform certain immodest acts he required, this cunning brute relieved us of both our cash and our cake. We'd been planning to bring three sheets of red velvet to my maiden aunt in Memphis, on the occasion of her eightieth."

Arin sat back in the bean bag chair, and after a moment Rell did the same. The warmth of Arin's body beside her was welcome, reassuring. Beside them, a candle flickered on a box drum. Rell held her hand above it, tasting its heat.

"At the moment we were sunk in deepest despair," the Devil said, "there appeared beside the payphone the fair figure of a fellow traveler—a Deadhead, by the look of him. In transit betwixt Vermont and Nevada, he offered to fetch us a few miles. But before the cheroot he'd lit had been stubbed out on the dash, our hero had veered south on sixty-five. Eight hours later, he deposited us on my dear Aunt Eleanor's doorstep."

"His name was Dyson," said the Freak. "Dyson saved us from Tyson."

"Though at that point," the Geek interjected, "we still knew him as Chris."

The Devil continued, unperturbed. "We didn't see him again until '95, at the Nevada Test Site protests. He was homeless, heartbroke, and his hair had gone gray. He was on his way to Frisco, but we managed to waylay him in Nederland at our family estate, home to ten or so degenerates, adjacent the Boulder National."

Here the Geek assumed narration, rubbing one hairy forearm as he spoke. "We'd had this circus flophouse for years, but inside of a week, Chris noticed something no one else had: the little blue pickup at the end of the street was abandoned.

Our neighbors had assumed it was ours, and we'd assumed it was theirs. Turns out, it belonged to a guy named Dyson Lathe."

"Alas," said the Devil, "we discovered this after we broke in."

Rell felt Arin's energy shift, though her posture was still relaxed. She was listening intently.

The Freak clicked the stud through his tongue against his teeth—thoughtfully, perhaps—once, twice, and again. "Dyson Lathe—the real Dyson Lathe—was an artist. The whole truck was filled with his drawings of birds. Pages and pages of birds, all of them either extinct or endangered. He'd copied old lithograpghs or worked from photographs, though the guy didn't seem to have any formal training; it was just something he did. There were stacks of books in his truck on how to identify edible plants and survive in the wild." The Freak looked over at the Geek. "But wherever Dyson Lathe had gone, he'd left all that behind."

The Devil arched one elegant eyebrow. "His wallet as well."

"We called the number on the driver's license," the Geek told them. "The girl who answered turned out to be the guy's roommate. Said nobody had heard from him in over a year. His mother had figured he was dead."

The Freak looked solemnly around the circle. "His mother didn't want any of his possessions. Not even his art. Either she didn't care or she couldn't handle it. She told us to keep the truck."

No one had moved since the story began. Jenna's banjo lay at her side, Crockett's arm around her shoulders, as she looked off into the shadows; Crockett appeared lost in thought, gazing into the depths of the threadbare Oriental carpet that covered the floor of the bus. Natalie sat with Michelle, staring at the candle on the box drum, which wavered in a breeze, now and then, from no discernible source, the breath of ghosts among them.

"Chris Mason kept that little Nissan, along with the guy's ID. He looked enough like Dyson Lathe that he started using that driver's license when he went out to the bar, and eventually, when he got a job with our friend's nonprofit, the guy's social security number as well." The Geek, dark and swarthy in the guttering candlelight, looked increasingly like the Greek. "After a while we were the only ones in our scene who'd ever known him as Chris, and there was sort of a point where we figured out that Chris had done something back in Eugene that he needed to distance himself from."

The Devil lifted a finger. "That point arrived when a former intimate of his came through on tour, with a band of the hardcore persuasion. They were known as No Compromise." He pursed his lips. "A name that would prove ultimately ironic."

The Freak's face, which was long to begin with, now seemed even longer. "Our old buddy Chris would probably still be here today if we hadn't run into him back in Boulder last year. He told us he'd started an infoshop in Crest Top, his old college town." The Freak shot a look at the Geek. "Which, in retrospect, he would have been wiser not to."

"He wanted us to come down here and perform," said the Geek. "But by then, we'd already booked an East Coast tour."

Michelle smiled. It was a faraway smile, both hard and soft, beneath the bleached-out unicorn horn of her bangs. "You guys were his favorite assholes in the world."

"Truth!" said the Freak. "She speaks the truth!"

"And you fucking missed him."

The Devil looked off. Flecks of gel had appeared in his pompadour, beads of sweat on his brow. "But old Uncle Sam had a plan for our man. Who happened to have a hand in blowing a dam."

"A terrible dam," said the Freak, "benefitting no one but the man."

"It was a damned bad dam," the Geek agreed.

"As well as, it must be said, a cheerful conflagration or two. But now," the Devil said, with a gay wave, "it appears we've arrived too late. Our old friend Christopher Mason has joined Dyson Lathe in that great walk off into the sky."

Softly, Crockett whistled, and Jenna smiled, looking a bit misty. At what, Rell couldn't quite say, though she could not help but think of Katie then, the way she'd stepped over the ridge that day in Wind Valley, as if into the wild blue beyond.

Arin was leaning into her, into this space they'd created. Rell leaned back, releasing her weight, and their heads touched. They were sitting close now, like girlfriends, like lovers. The campfire was aglow inside Rell, and she felt as if they had always known each other.

The Geek raised a toast of the two-buck chuck that had appeared at some point in the evening. "And so we say unto you, brethren, sistren, heed this cautionary tale. Take care of one another. Love one another, and make family of friends." He looked around the circle and held each eye in turn. "And above all," he said, "beware of old punks with good teeth and new shoes. You never know who you might lose."

The Devil leaned in. "So saith," the three performers intoned in unision, "the Dead Man's Revival."

A moment of silence hung suspended in what seemed an echo of accordion music. But the Devil's accordion lay still beside him. How could there be two accordions on the same street on the same night? What the hell were the chances of that?

"To Chris Mason," said the Freak, holding aloft the hellacious jug.

"To Dyson Lathe," said the Geek.

"To all the fallen," the Devil said, and everyone murmured agreement.

In the circle of friends sprawled out on pillows, no one moved. The energy was no longer light, but still sweet, like the desert slipping slowly into sunset. Everyone seemed suddenly lost in some separate place.

About the Author

SUSAN DEFREITAS was raised in rural west Michigan and spent fourteen years in the high desert of central Arizona. She is a graduate of Prescott College and Pacific University; her fiction, nonfiction, and poetry has been published in over thirty journals, magazines, and anthologies. She works as an freelance editor in Portland, Oregon, where she lives with her husband and their bad circus cat. This is her first novel.

Hot Season: A Reader's Group Guide

An interview with the author and questions designed to enrich your book club discussions are available online at www.susandefreitas.com

Acknowledgments

This book bears a debt of gratitude to Thisbe Nissen, who was my mentor at Pacific University when I wrestled my way through many of the first drafts that would become the chapters of this book. And to Benjamin Percy, who wanted to see something blow up: while you didn't make the prospect of defending my thesis any less terrifying, your feedback did help to shape this book.

Many thanks are due to some of my closest literary accomplices, Lisa Galloway and Tabitha Blankenbiller, and to Alissa Hattman most especially for reading this manuscript in several indeterminate states and encouraging me, always, to stick with it. ("It works. It's good!") To the members of my writing group, the Guttery: Thank you for your unflagging support as I've launched this book into the world.

And finally, all thanks and praise to Daniel—my husband, first reader, cheerleader, ceaseless source of joy and encouragement in this world, and above all, my friend.

More books from Harvard Square Editions:

Augments of Change, Kelvin Christopher James

Gates of Eden, Charles Degelman

Love's Affliction, Fidelis Mkparu

Transoceanic Lights, S. Li

Close, Erika Raskin

Anomie, Jeff Lockwood

Living Treasures, Yang Huang

Nature's Confession, J.L. Morin

A Face in the Sky, Greg Jenkins

Dark Lady of Hollywood, Diane Haithman

Fugue for the Right Hand, Michele Tolela Myers

Growing Up White, James P. Stobaugh

The Beard, Alan Swyer

Parallel, Sharon Erby